Best MAN

new york times bestselling author
KATY EVANS

First paperback edition: December 2019

Cover design by Sara Hansen at Okay Creations
Interior formatting by JT Formatting

10 9 8 7 6 5 4 2 1

Library of Congress Cataloguing-in-Publication Data is available

ISBN-13: 978-1-7324439-3-8
ISBN-13: (ebook)978-1-7324439-2-1

table of contents

11	6:34 PM, December 6	87
12	9:06 PM, December 6	102
13	11:36 PM, December 6	116
14	2:06 AM, December 7	135
15	3:10 AM, December 7	151
16	3:30 AM, December 7	159
17	4:02 AM, December 7	172
18	5:02 AM, December 7	184
19	6:18 AM, December 7	187
20	7:08 AM, December 7	193
21	9:28 AM, December 7	200
22	10:38 AM, December 7	205
23	11:00 AM, December 7	208
24	11:16 AM, December 7	217
25	11:25 AM, December 7	222

11:00 AM, DECEMBER 7

The dress is a strapless Carolina Herrera, with layers and layers of whisper-thin organza. It blows my budget and the "less is more" mantra out of the water, but like Eva said the day we bought it in downtown Denver, *when you know, you know*. The locale is the sumptuous Midnight Lodge, nestled in Colorado's Rocky Mountains, every tiny detail of the place costing my father more than an entire year of his salary. The twenty-three members of the bridal party are assembled. It's the scene of every little girl's fairytale fantasy.

My fantasy.

At least, the one I'd been harboring up until today, when everything changed.

Eva smiles at me. "Ready to make your dreams come true?"

I stare at myself in the mirror. I look like Cinderella, if the wicked stepmother had just materialized at the castle on Cinderella's wedding day and gunned down Prince Charming in cold blood. I'm also about three minutes away from losing the mimosa I'd polished off earlier that morning at breakneck speed. I go to chew on my nails but then I remember Eva painted them, and the last thing I want is for him to see the chips.

He notices things like that. He's an observer.

And I want to be perfect for him.

Him.

The wrong him.

Oh, god.

I go to chew on my lip, but I can't do that because they've been lacquered with bubble-gum pink gloss, and he'd probably notice if I got it on my teeth, too. All my normal ways of freaking out are off limits.

This is the day of my dreams, the day I've planned to the letter, just so I could avoid any potential calamities that might make me freak out.

But I *am* freaking out. Oh, lordy, am I ever.

I've been waiting my whole life for this day.

This perfect day, where the sun is shining, the snow is melting, birds are singing, and the sky is the deepest blue I've ever seen.

But there's a problem.

A problem in the form of a pretentious, bearded, six-foot-three wall of hot man flesh who stalks around hating the world and thinking he's better than everyone in it.

My fiancé's best friend. The best man, Miles Foster.

This is all his fault.

"You okay?" Eva asks.

"I am," I insist, pushing the infernal veil out of my face for the thousandth time. "This dress is itchy as hell."

I stand and pluck the dress up under my armpits, hoisting it over my boobs. I try to take a step but…too much fabric, in all directions. It's a wonder I don't drown in this sea. In this sea, or in this mess I've created for myself. I sit back down on the vanity stool and pout. "I'm stuck."

In more ways than one.

She gathers handfuls of too much organza and helps me up, depositing the pile of fabric safely in my wake. I shuffle to the full-length mirror and glance at myself. I don't look like a bride, or even a fairytale princess. I look like a prisoner who just got her death sentence.

"It's too loose," I whine. I never had much of a rack, and now it's super obvious. Why did I decide to go strapless again? "I think I must've lost some boobage during my diet. What if the top of my dress falls down while I'm walking up the aisle?"

Eva smirks. "I'm sure Aaron'll love the show."

The thought makes the mimosa turn in my stomach. I used to live for what Aaron thought. Whenever I had a choice to make on something, be it a new movie coming out, or a sweater at the mall, or a new hair style, I'd think, *Would Aaron like this?* But I realize, as she says his name, that it doesn't matter to me in the slightest what Aaron thinks. The only opinion I care about now is that of the man who will be standing precisely two feet to my husband-to-be's left.

I am such an idiot.

In less than fifteen minutes, I will be marching down the stone steps outside the Midnight Lodge to a picturesque gazebo at the foot of the hills, on the arm of my father, who has socked his entire life's savings into making this day picture perfect for his only daughter. I will take the hand of the man I've been attached at the hip to for over five years, ever since I met him in a dank frat cellar when I was a wide-eyed little college freshman. I will join with this man—this man I've spent all of my adult life with—in holy matrimony, 'til death us do part.

I will become Mrs. Aaron Eberhart.

But I know I'll be looking past my husband-to-be to the man who, up until twelve hours ago, I'd thought I hated. Miles Foster.

And I will be wondering *What if...*

I wish choosing a husband was as simple as choosing a dress.

When you know, you know.

I *did* know, or I thought I did. Up until twelve hours ago, I thought Aaron Eberhart was my true soul mate, the one I'd happily spend the rest of my life with. That's when things took an unexpected turn.

Right now? I don't even know my own name.

And I have a feeling I might be making a huge mistake.

9:00 AM, DECEMBER 6

E va knocks on the door to my hotel room and screams so the entire lodge can hear, "Happy Wedding Day Eve!"

I grin as my fairytale princess dreams dissolve in my head, and I'm faced with the reality, which is, for once, even better.

I'm fucking getting married.

I sit up in my little double bed and blink in the sunlight. Tomorrow night, my wedding night, I'll share the spectacular Presidential Suite with my husband. Just me and my husband and a massive king bed with silk sheets.

And sex. Lots of hot, wedding-night sex.

My pulse flutters when I think of my hotter fiancé, Aaron. We've been together half a decade, had sex probably a thousand times. But sex as man and wife...it's got to be different, right? Hotter, more intense?

I shiver again just thinking of it. Of being a wife. To Aaron.

Ohmigod.

I'm twenty-three, and in just over twenty-four hours, I will be Mrs. Aaron Eberhart!

I scramble out of bed, doing a little dance of excitement, and tear open the door, a big grin on my face. Eva has her blonde hair in a loop atop her head and is wearing Lycra pants and a hoodie, straight outta eight AM yoga. She's also holding a bag of Danishes and two big traveler mugs of coffee. "And how's my favorite bride?" she sings.

I rub my hands together and grab the coffee. "Great. Tell me this is black."

"What kind of best friend do you think I am? After twenty years of being besties, I think I know how you take your coffee." She opens the bag and pulls out a round Danish, laying it on a napkin. She sits down at the little table and pulls her knees up to her chest, biting into a raspberry. "Danish?"

I wrinkle my nose as I sip the coffee. "I have a dress to fit into, remember?"

"Really? For what?" she asks with mock confusion. Then she smiles. "Just take a whirl on the elliptical downstairs later. Hope you're ready to spa yourself silly today."

"Oh, yes. I'm so in. I need to do something to these nails."

I hold them out and she inspects them. They're practically chewed to the quick because of all the nervous energy I have. I'm an awful nail-chewer.

"Yikes. You definitely need a mani-pedi. Your dad's paying for anything we want done?" She reaches into her gym bag and pulls out the Midnight Lodge Spa brochure. "Because I think I'm doing the chocolate and champagne decadence massage and body facial."

I shrug. "He said, and I quote, 'It isn't every day my only daughter gets married. Treat yourself!' My mom's doing the works. But chocolate and champagne? I think I gained ten pounds just hearing that."

She eyes my body, which I've been beating into submission with PiYo classes and endless dieting since Aaron proposed, nineteen months ago. "You look great."

I spin around in front of the full-length mirror, zeroing in on my butt in the boxers I'm wearing. I've squatted enough to give myself a little shelf back there, and I hardly jiggle at all anymore. "I'm so excited. I can't wait to see Aaron's jaw drop when he sees me. I keep dreaming about it."

She smiles. "Oh, he'll be unable to take his eyes off you."

I frown. The truth is, Aaron hasn't really noticed my transformation at all. But that's because I wear baggy clothes most of the time. In the dress, with the help of the corset to cinch my waist and push up my boobs, it'll be obvious. "He better."

In my mind, the scene is set: The distant mountains, the crisp air, the robin's-egg-blue sky, loving family from far and wide. And up ahead, the man. The man of my dreams. I thrill for the thousandth time in an hour and grab a tank and yoga pants to change into, then knot my hair up on top of my head in a messy bun. "Ready!"

I'm excited to go downstairs. Because we've brought over five hundred guests in, it's almost like we own the place. Everywhere I look, there's someone I know and love. I hug some friends from college in the elevator, and when I get down to the lobby, a crew of cousins and aunts and people I don't even know begin to whistle the Wedding March. I grin and bow, blushing, and they all applaud.

I want to bottle this moment and keep it forever.

The only thing that would make it more perfect would be if Aaron was here with me.

But he's not. I scan the vast lobby but don't see him anywhere. Maybe he's at breakfast.

We cross past the floor-to-ceiling stone fireplace to the little restaurant, following the sounds of chattering and silverware clinking to a packed room. I look around and spot all ten of my bridesmaids, as well as the two flower girls and the ring bearer, sitting around a big circular table.

But no Aaron.

Eva and I go over to my bridal party. While Natalie and Cara are good friends from high school that Eva and I both know, the others are distant family members and even some of Aaron's family, whom I don't know so well. But Aaron has so many friends—mostly frat brothers—that he couldn't narrow it down to less than ten, so in order to keep things even, I ended up asking people I barely knew.

I hug Natalie and Cara and wave at the others, then give my three little five-year-old triplet cousins kisses. "Hi! Everyone having fun? Ready for spa time at ten?"

They all nod, and the little girls, wearing matching "flower girl" tank tops, clap their hands. I hug them tight and kiss their chubby cheeks again. "You two are going to look so beautiful!" I gush.

Natalie gives a whoop. She says, "Hey, girl. You hear about the bachelor party?"

Uh-oh. I'm not sure I want to. The skin on the back of my neck prickles. "What about it?"

"Nothing. Just that Mike didn't get home until six."

Mike is her husband. He seemed kind of sedate when I met him, which I'd thought was a good thing. Aaron's claim to fame is rocking the roof off parties, so I hoped a couple of sticks in the mud would prevent him from getting out of hand.

Or so I thought.

"In the morning?" I blurt stupidly.

She nods.

I straighten. Well, that explains why Aaron is MIA. But I don't get it. The bachelor party yesterday was skiing at Winter Park. Then they were maybe going to have a few beers and chill out. A little low-key après-ski fun, Aaron had said, nothing too wild.

But six in the morning? That sounds…worrisome. I can't help but get a sinking feeling in my stomach. "What? What did they do?"

She shrugs. "They went to some club. I don't know. But when he came in, he smelled like a brewery, and then he started puking all over the bathroom."

"A club? That doesn't sound low-key." I rub my temples, still unable to shake the sinking feeling brought on by memories of Old School Aaron.

The Aaron he promised he'd left behind. Because he loves me.

Oh, god.

Noticing my alarm, Eva reaches out and jiggles my arm. "I'm sure it's fine."

I'm *not* so sure.

Aaron used to pride himself on being the ultimate party guy. If a friend did a keg stand, he'd do two. If a brother danced on the bar in their D-Phi cellar, he'd do it naked. His frat nickname was Guppy, because he drank like a fish, *all the time.*

He always had to push the limits, especially when alcohol was involved.

We used to have all these fights because he wouldn't ever turn away from any woman who flirted with him. Because sometimes he did worse than flirt—when he was drunk.

I look at Natalie. "Did Mike say anything…about Aaron?"

She gives me an apologetic shrug. "No. Sorry."

I stay quiet, realizing I'm the hostess and this isn't a good time to have a freak-out, but the second I can break away, I dial Aaron's cell.

It goes right to voicemail.

I dial it again, expecting a different result, but no. Voicemail again.

All sorts of cringeworthy images start to bloom in my head. Winter Park was probably full of cute little ski bunnies in tight outfits, and Aaron has always had an eye for pretty women.

More than an eye when he's drunk, which was what inspired our last breakup.

Oh, gosh, relax, Lia! You're overreacting.

That was nineteen months ago, before he grew up, proposed, and became a changed man. Sure he still drinks, but other than that, he's a virtual saint, now. I just hope he didn't overdo it in the drinking department and hurt himself.

I quickly jab in a text: *U ok?*

I stare at the text, willing him to respond, but he doesn't. Then I look up and see a kind, familiar face, smiling at me across the restaurant.

It's my ninety-year-old Mimi, my great-grandmother, from Sacramento. I haven't seen her in years.

I almost run over a waiter carrying a full tray of breakfast on my dash to her. I'm bawling by the time I get there. She's dressed to the nines, as usual, in a polyester pink suit, with pink lipstick to match. Her hair is dyed platinum—she looks like Barbie as a grandmother. I hug her excitedly. "Mimi! I'm getting married!"

"I know, sweetheart," she says in her soft but gravelly voice as I crouch in front of her table. "You look positively glowing, Dahlia. I couldn't miss my favorite great-grandchild's big day."

I'm not her favorite great-grandchild; all of us are. She has about thirty great-grandchildren scattered about the country and never misses a birthday for any of them. I know the tears I'm crying will probably blotch up my face, but I can't help it. "I'm so glad you came."

"Of course! Though I really thought I'd be coming in for Weston's wedding, first. What happened to him?"

I look around for my older brother, West. He was invited to the bachelor party festivities last night, but had said he was "beyond" that, considering he'd just turned thirty. Plus, the guy's always working. It's a shame. He would've made a nice fly on the wall for me. "Oh. Well, he's probably at the gym. Or working. You know him."

She gives her head a disappointed shake. "Does he even have a girlfriend?"

I shake my head. West has lots of girls. So many, I've lost track. He eats them up and spits them out like sport. "No one special."

"Ah, that's a shame. He's so handsome. Speaking of handsome, where is your fiancé? Aaron, is it? I hear he's quite the dish. I'd like to meet him."

"Oh, yes." I gnaw on my lip a little, until I realize that's probably not good for my overall look, either. "He had a late night with his bachelor party, but he'll be around shortly. How was your flight? Can you believe this place? Your grandson went all-out on this."

"It's just fine." She looks around, her lips puckering in distaste. "Yes. It's quite nice. But you know, it isn't so much the event as it is the man, don't you think?"

"Yes. Of course. I mean—"

"All this stuff is nice, but," she leans in closer, as if she's about to tell me some great Mimi wisdom, "it's not really necessary, is it?"

"Well...no. But it's a once-in-a-lifetime thing, right? Might as well do it right."

"Right? Your great-grandfather and I got married at city hall and shared a funnel cake on the boardwalk in Santa Monica. That was right for us," she says, her eyes misting a little, likely caught in the memory.

I smile and pat the wax-paper-thin skin on the back of her hand. That's nice and all, but Aaron and I agreed on this: Go big or go home. He loves parties. Lives for parties. And I want something people will remember. This is the way to do it. I've been planning this forever. This is right for us.

I straighten and say, "Well, I'll be sure to introduce you to Aaron when he comes down. Are you coming to spa day?"

She shakes her head. "Oh, no. That's for you young girls."

"You're young!"

She waves a hand at me. "Oh, go on, Dahlia."

"Okay, well...I'll see you later?"

She nods. "Have fun, sweetheart."

I hug her, inhaling her too-sweet Jean Nate, then go off to find Eva and the rest of the girls waiting for me.

I check my phone. The appointment's at ten and we have about fifteen minutes to get down there. I can just imagine sitting in a mud bath, immobile, fretting over what Aaron's up to and whether he's drowning in a pool of his own vomit. That'll be really relaxing.

"Eva, you know...why don't you take the girls down there and get started? I'm just going to go up and check on Aaron."

She wrinkles her nose. "Are you sure?"

I wave her away. "Yes. I'm sure. I'll just be a few minutes."

I take the elevator up to the second floor, find his room, and knock on the door. I listen. Nothing.

I knock louder.

Oh, great. He's been the responsible, model boyfriend for the past nineteen months...and he picks *now* to go wild?

I knock until my knuckles start to ache.

Nothing.

"Whoa. Bridezilla. Chill out."

I cringe at the sound of the deep baritone behind me. That can only belong to one person in the entire world.

I whirl around to see Miles. All six-feet-plus-plenty-more-inches of him. My face automatically twists into a scowl. That's the effect my fiancé's best friend has on me.

I cross my arms, trying my best to ignore the fact that he's shirtless and drenched, his board shorts clinging to his defined thigh muscles. He has a towel slung over one shoulder and his dark hair is spiky with water. Miles Foster is, in every sense of the word, perfection.

And he knows it.

Smug bastard.

His room is right across the hall from Aaron's. He stops there and reaches into his pocket, so I get a view of his broad back. Yep, perfection from that side, too. Not a freaking blemish, and muscles to make a girl weep, his spine and the dimples on his lower back making a perfect arrow pointing right to his ass.

I have very little memory of our first night together, but what I *do* remember? I don't want to remember. Not at all, and yet I do. Remember. *Stuff.* Like… his ass is like a squeeze toy. Once you get it in your hands, you simply. Can't. Stop.

It's unfair that God felt the need to grace an asshole with such gifts.

"You're dripping all over the floor, dumbass," I say to him.

He finds his key card and swipes it, pushing open the door to his room. He's ignoring me, something he's gotten very good at over the five years we've known each other.

He saunters inside and is about two seconds from slamming his door on me when I shout out, "Wait!"

He holds the door and turns in a leisurely way, stroking scruff that is forever bordering on a full-on beard. "Yeah?"

I point behind me. "Little help?"

He leans casually against the doorjamb, takes the end of his towel, and rubs it through his hair so it gets spikier. Little droplets spray me in the face. Jerk. "What?"

"Well…" I let out an exasperated sigh. "You were out with him last night, weren't you? Is he in there? Is he okay? I have five hundred guests downstairs and they're beginning to wonder about him."

His lips twist in amusement. "Yes. I was with him. Yes, we skied, and then we went to a club. Yes, we got home late.

And yes, he's okay. So stop worrying, Bridezilla. You have twenty-four hours until the blessed event of the year. Your perfect wedding will go off without a hitch, I'm sure."

My scowl deepens. "Is it too much to want to see him myself? Speak to him?"

He crosses the hallway and comes up close to me, so I can smell the chlorine from his swim, see the green flecks in the angry-storm-blue irises of his eyes. I'm more than a foot shorter than him, a fact that's never been so obvious as it is now when he's towering over me with all his naked gorgeousness on full display.

I nearly choke on my breath.

The door clicks closed behind him. "Don't you have a seaweed wrap or some other form of torture to put yourself through, which you think will make you look better for tomorrow but will in fact do absolutely nothing noticeable but drain your daddy's wallet?"

"I..." That is Miles' power. He lives to strike people speechless. He's ridiculously perceptive, the way he reaches into a person's soul like that and strikes all the right chords. He's like some kind of wizard that way. He's the kind of guy who goes his own way, and at first, you think he's nuts, and then you start to realize he's actually brilliant as fuck. I hate that about him. "What? Look, I just want to talk to Aaron. My fiancé."

He's looking into my eyes, assessing me with that same superiority that makes me feel about three inches tall. And then he says, "You need to get your nails done."

I look down. Yes, my nails are atrocious. But how did he know? Had he even looked at my nails? And what kind of guy goes around peeking at women's fingernails?

I ball my hands into fists, dangerously close to punching him.

Probably not a good way to feel, twenty-five hours before my wedding. With my luck, I'll end up breaking my hand on all his glorious hardness, and what a great honeymoon in Maui that'll be.

I skirt away from him and back down the hallway. "Look. Can you just have him call me when you get him up? He really needs to be downstairs, stat. Thanks."

I walk quickly, my skin crawling all over from the encounter. I know his eyes are on me, following my every step away from him.

I can't believe that he…and I… once…

Ugh. That is not something to think about on the eve of my marriage to his best friend.

I wonder if the Midnight Lodge Spa has delousing treatments.

9:49 AM DECEMBER 6

Ugh. Miles Foster.

It's amazing Aaron and I survived this long, considering I absolutely despise his choice of best friend. Miles is almost a deal-breaker, he's that bad. To think, during that first CU Boulder frat party I ever went to, I'd looked at all the fraternity brothers across the dank, hazy cellar, and zeroed in on him.

Right. So did every other girl in the basement.

Where Aaron is the all-American blond, Miles is his dark underside. He's unbearably hot, scorching even.

But the hotness drains away whenever he opens his mouth.

Unfortunately, neither of us spoke much that first night, or maybe I'd have been warned. It was my first college party and, hyped on the feeling of freedom, I'd gone a little overboard in the drinking department. The music was too loud, and we were all too smashed.

How was I to know that one little night of fun would send such huge shockwaves through my life?

So I did what I had to do. I buried it. And so did he. Knowing him, and the way he treats me and every other woman who comes into his orbit, he probably doesn't even remember it.

As I hurry downstairs to the spa, still shaking off the hee-bie-jeebies my every encounter with Miles seems to bring, I nearly laugh, thinking of what he'd said to me. Really, what kind of lame idiot guy cares about a girl's nails? And Bridezilla? Please.

Par for the course, I think. I should know better than to let him get under my skin. Miles has never greeted me with a, "Hey, how's it going?" It's always, "If it isn't Shorty," or "What are you looking at, Headcase?" So I shouldn't have been too hurt by, "Whoa. Bridezilla. Chill out."

He's a douche beyond all reason. And somehow, Aaron's bestie. It's just awful.

But if I want Aaron, I guess I have to take his good *and* bad. Marriage is about compromise and acceptance. After all, it's in the vows: for better or for worse.

Miles definitely qualifies as the latter. The only saving grace is that lately, with Miles working and living in down-town Denver and us up in Boulder, and area traffic being what it is, and our schedules being what they are, we rarely get a chance to hang with Miles much anymore. This past year, we'd gone out for dinner and drinks a couple of times.

Deciding to force any thoughts of the idiot best friend out of my head for the rest of my stay, I make it down to the basement and find Eva, who's already sprawled out on a towel, in the midst of her champagne and chocolate body facial. All I've had is that black coffee, so the smell of chocolate is mak-ing my mouth water.

She lifts her chin and gazes at me with blissfully sleepy eyes. "You find him?"

I shake my head and remind myself for the thousandth time to stop gnawing on my lip. The last thing I want is to be chapped for my first kiss with Aaron as a married couple.

"Don't worry. I'm sure he's fine."

"That's what the best man said when I ran into him." I make a face.

She groans. She has heard all my stories about what an absolute douchebucket Miles is, *except* for the one where we ended up... Nope, not thinking about it.

"What's his problem, anyway? I complimented his ski jacket when he came in yesterday and he told me not to touch him."

I raise an eyebrow. "Did you try?"

"Well, you know me."

I do. Eva is notoriously touchy-feely, and Miles is notoriously not. He must have OCD, because he hates people touching his things, getting in his space. Aaron is the biggest slob on earth, and he said Miles' room in the frat house—he couldn't have a roommate because he was too anal—was like a museum. There's a reason his frat nickname was Sergeant Shitface—he does everything with military precision. And if you brush his arm or anything? He goes batshit. It's hard to believe, considering he and I had been *very* cozy when—

Ugh! For the last time, don't think about that!

"I told you not to! He's so weird like that!"

She sighs. "Yes. He's such a weird asshole. What is he, a germaphobe or something? But god...he's hot. So hot."

"And he knows it," I mutter, as my phone starts to buzz. I lift it. It's my sweetie. I pick it up and purr, "Hi. Are you okay?"

Eva watches me carefully as I hear a gravelly voice say, "Yeah. Hey, babe. What's up?"

"Nothing, but what's up with you? I was worried when I didn't see you downstairs. People are asking about you."

"I'm good. Just a late night last night. You know. The boys wanted to keep it going. Last hurrah, you know?"

I let out a little laugh. "Sure, I get it. Well, I'm glad you went out last night instead of tonight. You'll be okay for the wedding, right?"

"Oh, sure, hon. Of course," he says in a sexy, low growl that makes me wish I could be with him right now. "But I have a slight problem."

I grit my teeth. I don't want slight problems. Everything is supposed to be perfect. I'm not sure if my nerves can take *any* problems, even slight ones. "What?"

"You know the rings?"

Rings. Rings. He says it so dismissively, surely he can't be talking about the platinum rings that are the core symbol of our enduring union. I try to think of some other meaning for some other description for them. But I can't.

I gaze down at the engagement ring we purchased together nineteen months ago—platinum setting, pear-shaped solitaire. He wasn't sure what I'd like so when he proposed, he did it without the ring, and we went out shopping later. "You mean the wedding rings?"

"Yeah. I seem to have…"

Oh, no. No no no.

My heart is in my throat, and it's precisely because I know what kind of guy Aaron is. He's fly-by-the-seat-of-his-pants. He doesn't plan. In fact, all the planning that's been done for this wedding has been mine. If I'd relied on *him*, we'd never have set a date.

Case in point: I'd had my suitcase for this trip, and one for our honeymoon in Hawaii, packed for three weeks. He packed his suitcases five minutes before we left, and it was like a clothing bomb hit his apartment.

"Aaron. Please don't tell me you forgot the rings," I whisper.

A pause. Then: "I forgot the rings."

"NOOOOOOOOOO!" I gasp, so loud and long that everyone in the spa stares at me, and the woman covering Eva's thighs with melted chocolate drops her brush. The two girl triplets, who are getting manicures, start to cry. "No. No. No. Please, tell me you're just joking!"

"I wish I was, honey," he says, entirely too calm for my liking. "But don't worry. They're a symbol. They don't mean anything. We can just, I don't know, use some fish hooks or chicken wire or whatever."

For a moment, I feel struck. Like he actually punched me. In the heart. My groom didn't actually just suggest to me that we get married exchanging chicken wire, did he?

I thought I loved him. Now, I'm not so sure.

"Aaron..." I'm trying to stay calm, but bile rises up my throat. "This is *not* a slight problem. Are we going to go back and get them?" I ask, checking the clock on the wall. "If we leave now...five hours there and five hours back...we can be back by the rehearsal dinner."

He lets out a raspy breath. "Shit, Lia. I wish I could, but...I'm still drunk. My head's pounding. I just popped two Excedrin but I don't know when they'll kick in."

I'm gripping the phone against my ear so hard I'm surprised I don't crush that side of my skull. I look wildly around, then set my jaw. "Okay. Here's what we do. I'll go get them."

"Hon, no, you don't need to put yourself through—"

"Stop. Seriously. There's no time to lose. Just tell me where you left them."

"They're in my night sta—" He stops. "Lia. Wait. Do you realize what you're saying? You can't—"

Noticing I'm drawing eyes, I move around so the girls don't overhear me, cupping the phone with my hand. "Aaron *please*. It's our *wedding*. We've planned this for forever and there's still *time*. I seriously don't want to express my love for you with something you use to impale fish."

Silence.

I shut my eyes, counting to three. But he still doesn't say anything. Nothing even remotely like: "Lia, honey, I'll get them. This will be the perfect wedding, baby, like we've always wanted."

Feeling a renewed sense of urgency that the wedding needs to be perfect, I mumble, "I'm coming up to get the keys to your apartment right now."

I punch the End Call button and notice everyone in the spa is staring at me, except for the little girls, who are covering their faces with their hands and sobbing a little.

"Minor setback," I say, managing a smile.

"You're not leaving, are you?" Natalie asks from behind her white facial mask, as the attendant fixes a cucumber on her lid.

Eva pushes up onto her elbows and pounds the table with her fists. "No. Hell no. This is an intervention! I refuse to let you drive all over creation the day before your wedding because your idiot fiancé dropped the ball! You should be relaxing and pampering yourself! Let one of the guys drive."

I shake my head. "They're all drunk."

"Well, what about West?"

"I have no idea where he is. And I can't trust any of them any more than I can trust Aaron right now." I shrug. "It's not a big deal. I have so much nervous energy, I'm jumping all over the place. It'll be good to have something to do. I don't mind."

Eva pouts. "But I do! You can't, Lia. You dreamed of this time. And what about the rehearsal dinner?"

"It's at eight tonight. I'll be back by then."

My mother appears in a fluffy white robe, her hair in a towel. "Honey, are you sure? Maybe you don't need the rings."

I shake my head. I can just imagine how great the photos will look—us wearing matching chicken wire as a symbol of our love. Fuck no. "I need the rings. He said they're right in his night table. And you know me, I was never one for massages and pampering and stuff, anyway. I'm good."

Besides, it'll do nothing noticeable but drain my daddy's wallet.

Ugh. Why the fuck am I taking into consideration what Sergeant Shitface thinks?

My mother comes around and massages my tense shoulders. "You can ask your father to go."

"Mom. No. You know he'd never go above fifty, even if he saw the apocalypse approaching in his rearview mirror. This is not a big deal," I repeat. "Trust me."

I hug all my family and bridesmaids and rush upstairs to get my bag and keys. As I'm zipping up my hoodie and slipping my sunglasses on while walking towards Aaron's room to pick up his apartment keys, I see a tall, lean figure down the hall.

It's Sergeant Shitface, himself.

He's dressed in an open flannel shirt, jeans, and a wool skullcap, and is tossing something up into the air, catching it with one hand. If he had an ax, he'd be a ridiculously hot Paul Bunyan.

"You know there's a snowstorm coming, right, genius?"

Annnnd the scowl is back. "Don't talk to me about the weather. I've been monitoring the weather like Jim Freaking Cantore, considering I have a little thing called an outdoor wedding coming up. You may have heard of it?"

He smirks. "So you really think you're going to get to Boulder and back before it hits?"

"Yes. Of course. It's just a little squall, and it'll be coming after nightfall. It'll only last two hours, providing a light dusting, so it'll be bright and sunny for go-time. The patio is going to be set with my mauve Pantone Color 511 and cream Pantone Color 5035 napkins and twelve industrial-strength heat lamps, and there will be no snow at all by then. Snow is NOT invited. I hereby banish snow from the discussion from here on out." I open the weather app on my phone and shove it under his nose to prove it, careful not to touch him.

He doesn't look at it, just keeps smirking at me in that superior way, like he knows better.

God, I hate him.

I try to walk past him to Aaron's room, but then he dangles whatever was in his hand in front of me. It's Aaron's apartment keys. I try to grab them but he snatches them away and wags a finger at me like I'm a naughty schoolgirl. "No touch. I'll take care of these."

I stare at him until realization dawns. "You are not coming with me."

"Yeah, I am."

Ugh. The thought makes my stomach turn. I'd rather drive the route with a rabid dog in my passenger seat. "No way."

"Tough. I'm not letting you go alone."

He's got to be kidding me. "But we hate each other. We'll probably murder each other before we get over the mountain, careen off one of the cliffsides, and the next time they find us, we'll be nothing but a pair of skeletons with our bony hands wrapped around each other's necks."

He nods, agreeing. "Possible. But your fiancé asked me to take care of you. I'm sure I can put aside my homicidal desires where you're concerned for ten hours."

"Good for you," I mutter, spinning away from him and hoisting my purse onto my shoulder. "But I'm not sure *I* can."

10:23 AM DECEMBER 6

One-night stands are really a huge mistake.

Not that I'm an expert in them.

I've only had one in my life.

I'd been a freshman at CU, staying in the dorms, and aside from a couple of acquaintances I'd gone to high school with, I knew no one. I'd gotten the course catalogue, with the hundreds of majors to choose from. So many possibilities. It struck me at once that I didn't have to be Dahlia Ripley, the massive bookworm with the hopelessly mediocre SAT scores, the solid B-average, and the life resume that showed I'd done absolutely nothing meaningful or stand-out within the first eighteen years of my existence.

I could be anyone.

Spurred on by that thrilling prospect, during the first week of school, I really put myself out there, adopting Eva's modus operandi. I was the social butterfly. As uncomfortable as it was at first, I got to know every one of the girls on my floor in the all-girls dorm.

That first week of school, I did a lot of firsts.

When they started doing shots of Everclear, I was right there with them.

Smoking pot? Did that, too.

And (probably because of the Everclear and the pot), when word went around about the first frat party of the season that August, I was all-in for that little adventure, as well.

Delta Phi, right there on the corner of fraternity row, was the biggest, most imposing mansion on the block. When the school was founded, the university president had lived there, so it still bore symbols of late nineteenth-century elegance. According to the sophomores on my floor, it had the reputation for the best parties and the most gorgeous guys.

No kidding.

I felt like a kid in a candy store when I stepped down those crumbling stairs, into the crowd. The brothers at D-Phi were hot. Each one more gorgeous than the next. Older, too. They'd been around the college block before and now were masters of this domain. They stood lined up behind the dark, smoky basement bar, Solo cups of beer in hand, surveying each fresh-meat prospect as she walked in. Their gazes were nothing short of possessive, like, *You know you're not leaving here until you've sucked one of our dicks tonight.*

Well, all except one of them.

He was back farther than the rest, at the beer pong table. I didn't see him at first. I think if I had, I wouldn't have noticed anyone else.

But the other men gobbled us up as soon as we walked in. We were preening peacocks, a gaggle of shiny, nice-smelling hair, bare midriffs, short shorts, and girlish, drunken giggles. We'd soon learn we'd dressed too high school for college— that is, we cared too much about our appearance. Really, the only thing these men were looking for? Who would fall on her back and spread her legs the quickest.

The lines started.

What's your name? What's your major? You a freshman?

I answered those same questions about a thousand times, loving college. Loving life. Loving frat parties. Loving the attention.

Oh, the attention.

The wallflower at school, I'd have killed to be noticed by all the cute guys who walked the hallways. And I was being noticed here, under that dim cellar light, hands up in the air, slowly rotating my hips to some barely audible Chainsmokers song.

The attention brought out the monster in me. I felt invincible. I smiled seductively at all the men, looking at me, wanting me...

That was when I saw him.

He *wasn't* looking at me.

Which, of course, made me insanely curious.

The first thing I noticed was his dark hair, because he was almost directly under the bulb above him, and he was so tall that it cast what could only be called a supernatural aura, a halo, over the chiseled lines of his face. He arched one dark eyebrow in a skeptical way and his lips were pursed in thought. His light eyes narrowed in deep concentration at something in front of him. He was pitched forward a little, stroking his strong jaw pensively. Back then, he was clean-shaven.

He was beautiful.

All I knew was that I wanted to be whatever he was looking at. I craned my neck, hoping to see what amazing thing was holding him so rapt.

The place was too crowded, and more guys were surrounding me. *What's your major where you living how old are you?*

I swatted them away like flies. I was no longer interested in any of that.

As I shifted back and forth, I caught more glimpses. Broad shoulders, but not too broad. Athletic, but not brawny. He had more style than the hordes of guys in their rumpled, esoteric band t-shirts. He was wearing a plaid button-down shirt, wrinkle free. Somehow, he looked older, more mature.

He didn't belong down there, with them.

And suddenly, I didn't want to belong, either.

That's when the crowd parted a little, and I saw what was holding his attention.

Beer pong.

Oh.

But he was totally immersed in the game. He looked like he was trying to decode some cryptic message that the fate of the free world rested on, and yet...no. Just lame beer pong.

I remember being a little disappointed by that. He didn't look like the drinking game type. More like the Debate Club President, National Honor Society type.

He was watching one of the other guys, a cute—but totally lackluster—brother with a beer-stained D-Phi t-shirt, playing the game. The beautiful god leaned over and said something to the shorter guy, pointing out something on the board. The shorter guy nodded, threw the ball, and the place erupted in cheers. Some pathetic—and already too drunk—girl had to chug her beer.

I broke free of the crowd of brothers and headed to the edge of the table. I kept looking at the tall guy, but he never even blinked my way, even when I was standing just a few feet away. The shorter guy in the D-Phi shirt did, though.

He grinned. "I think we've got a new challenger."

Never having played beer pong in my life, I stepped back. "Oh, no! I'm just watching."

D-Phi Shirt Guy gave me a smirk. "Well. That's no fun. What's your name?"

"Lia."

He extended his hand. "I'm Aaron." He nudged the tall guy. "That's Miles."

Miles was still studying the beer pong table. Either he was really drunk or in some kind of zone. I started to say hi to him, but realized he wasn't paying attention.

Something inside me twisted. I desperately wanted him to look at me. The Everclear wasn't doing its job, because I wasn't as drunk as I needed to be, drunk enough not to care.

Aaron snapped his finger in Miles' face. Miles blinked, his eyebrows narrowing in annoyance, and caught sight of me. His gaze was so hot, I swear it sucked the air out of the room.

He ran a scrutinizing eye over me, his upper lip curled in a disgusted snarl. Suddenly, I felt like I was too insignificant to be breathing his air. "What's your name again?"

"Lia."

He let out a "hm" and went back to the game.

All right.

Fine.

Deflated, I looked at Aaron.

Aaron gave me a friendly smile that made up for his friend's lack of manners and muttered, "They don't call him Sergeant Shitface for nothing."

"Oh?"

"Yeah. We get names when we pledge. I'm Guppy."

He went into this story about how he'd come to be known as Guppy, and I only half-listened. I tried to keep my eyes on

Aaron, but I was still annoyed by his stuck-up, asshole of a friend. Really, what was his problem?

Where Miles wasn't a talker, his friend made up for it. Our first five minutes of conversation, I knew almost everything there was to know about Aaron. I knew that he was majoring in engineering, president of the fraternity and, based on the way people kept nudging him and giving him high-fives, the most popular guy in the place.

And he clearly liked me. "Hey. You want another beer? Let me get you a beer," he'd said, heading off toward the keg.

He left me with sullen, quiet, beer-pong-obsessed, but incredibly hot Miles.

And Miles didn't say a fucking word to me. He didn't even regard me like a piece of shit on the bottom of his shoe...because that would've required him to at least acknowledge my presence.

At that moment, I'd decided that I hated Miles Foster.

If only I'd spent all of that night thinking that.

Unfortunately, the beer was flowing and things wore on until dawn, and somehow—I'm trying to block out how—I ended up between the sheets in Miles' impeccable shrine-slash-bedroom.

Why oh why did I do that? If only I'd gone with my first instinct, which was that he was a total douchebucket.

Maybe then, this wouldn't be so totally uncomfortable.

Me. Miles. In my way-too-small Mini Cooper for the next ten hours. This time, though, I'm in total agreement with him. I don't want to say a word. Not a fucking syllable.

So I might as well go on record by saying this now: one-night stands are a huge mistake.

We're barely half a mile away from the Midnight Lodge. I can still see it in my rearview mirror. And Miles is already annoying me. His body fills up the passenger seat of the car, and because he's so tall, he's pushed the seat way back, meaning he's probably crushed all the stuff I keep in the back. He's popping his chewing gum and holding on to the strap over the window, giving me the distinct impression that he thinks I'm a bad driver. And he's wearing mirrored sunglasses in order to shut out the world he thinks he's better than.

At the exit of the lodge, it's nothing but flat earth as far as the eye can see, so I have good visibility down the highway as I come to the T intersection. There's a stop sign there, but because there are no cars coming either way, I make the left and ease out onto the highway without coming to a full stop.

He shakes his head.

Backseat driver.

"I'm a very good driver," I point out, trying to be cheerful.

"About as good as you are at chess."

Hmm. I'm a very good chess player, too. The problem is, he's better than I am. Not that we've played in a while. Not since my freshman year in college. We used to, all the time, in the library of the frat house, while everyone else was getting drunk. He beat me, every time. "Well…I'm not as obsessively competitive about it as you are. Freak."

"Riiight. Translation: You don't have a strategic mind."

I click my tongue. "You know, you were lucky you had me. I was too stupid to realize none of your brothers wanted to play against you because you were such a gloating asshole. Have you really found someone in Denver to willingly sign up for the torture?"

"Is that your way of asking if I have a girlfriend?"

I suck in my cheeks. "It's my way of asking if you have any friends whatsoever, or if you've managed to alienate the entire population of Denver."

He doesn't answer. So, yeah. Sergeant Shitface Did Denver, and no one there likes him, either.

Sometimes I'm amazed Aaron even made it into his small circle of friends. Actually, you can't really form a circle with one person. As far as I know, Aaron's the only person who likes Miles, probably because Aaron is so easy-going and likes everyone. Miles makes no secret of the fact that he likes absolutely *no one*, and so the feeling winds up being mutual.

"You play against the computer, don't you?" I laugh at him. "I bet even your computer can't stand your company. I bet you read dorky books about it in solitude. I bet you also bought a pipe so you can sit in front of the fireplace in your Denver apartment and watch Masterpiece Theater with a glass of sherry."

He's quiet for a while. But I haven't insulted him. He actually *likes* being a total oddball.

"I don't have a fireplace in my apartment."

"Hmm. I wouldn't know, considering how many times you've invited us there."

That shuts him up. It was a bone of contention for about three years, why he never asked us to visit him at his place, but now we just joke about it.

I have a country station on, blasting Thomas Rhett. I, like Aaron, love country music.

As I'm starting to bop my head and get into it, without asking, Miles leans over and switches the station. To—get this—some talk station. Some know-it-all guy, yammering on about the upcoming presidential election.

I switch it back. "I'm sorry. Did I say you could touch my radio?"

"It's not *your* radio," he says, switching it back to Mr. Boredom. "Didn't your daddy pay for this piece of shit?"

"Yes, but it was my graduation present, so the papers are in my name. And it's not a piece of shit."

"Fuck yes it is. It's a clown car. It's half a car."

"It's all I need."

"You? Judging from the circus back there at the lodge, you *need* a hell of a lot."

"I am not high-maintenance," I mumble. "Look at my nails, for god's sake."

"Trust me, I have." He picks a bit of imaginary dust off the dashboard, powers down the window, and flicks it out. "What does this car get? Like three miles to the gallon? And I bet it's shit in the snow."

"It's not. And we're not going to find out today. Because what did I tell you about the S word?" I switch it back to the country station with force and when he reaches for it again, I hold up a finger. "Touch that again and I'll kill you."

He reaches over like he's trying to caress it, getting me all tense. He moves his hand a hair away from every little button, but never actually touches them. He's doing this to play with me. What a fuckhead. "It *is* a piece of shit. Did you pick it out or did you lose a bet with your dad? I thought we were going in Aaron's Jeep."

I would swerve over to the shoulder and drop his ass there without a hint of regret, but that would waste precious time that I don't have.

"Listen to me. I don't like you. You don't like me. So just stay there, on the other side of the car, be quiet, and don't touch anything. Okay? And maybe we'll both survive this."

He snorts and crosses his arms. "Okay, Bridezilla. But *the other side of the car* in this piece of shit still has me almost in your lap."

"For the last time, I am *not* Bridezilla. And if I ever had the misfortune of you sitting in my lap, I would fucking gouge your eyes out."

"Whatever you say," he says flatly, looking out the window at the mountains in the distance, the ones we'll have to climb over in order to get to Aaron's apartment. The sun is so strong, it's making it really hot in the cabin, so I turn up the dial for the fan.

I will not attribute any of the heat to the man next to me. He may have been the source of some extremely…*adequate* sex, but that was in another lifetime. He's a douche squared, now.

When the fan's blowing, it's nice. I roll the window down a little, too. Right now, there isn't a cloud in the sky.

There's a squall due to arrive in a few hours? Right. The weathermen can go suck it.

He catches me looking at the sky and says, "It's coming."

"You're so wrong. Like I said, the S-word is not invited to this wedding."

"Yeah? So who made you God? I think the S-word at a wedding would be cool."

"Not my wedding. It's not happening. I fucking hate the S-word."

He lets out a short laugh. "It's a good thing you live in Colorado, then."

"Colorado isn't just about winter sports."

"Sure it is. The best skiing in the entire country is here. Have you ever put your feet in skis?"

I frown. "Ohhhh just shut up already."

The answer is no. I've never wanted to. My skin does weird shit in the cold. I hate the cold. Hate sports. But more than that, I was born with two left feet. When my dreams of becoming an Olympic ice-skating champion were dashed because I could barely stand upright in skates after a year of lessons, I figured there was no point in attempting skiing.

Unfortunately, the big ass next to me doesn't know the struggle. He was a killer rugby player in college, and nearly made the Olympic skiing and swim teams when he was at UC. And those are just the talents I know of, since I try not to pay attention. He's all sorts of special. I bet he's one of those people who excels at everything he tries.

As I'm thinking chicken wire might not be so bad an idea, he looks up from his phone. "So what I want to know is, whose genius idea was it for you two to get married on D-Day?"

Annnnd he's talking again. What about this whole thing about keeping quiet? I shush him.

Then his words suddenly hit me. "Wait, what?"

He smirks. "Do you even know that you're getting married on the day that will live in infamy?"

I give him a confused look over my sunglasses.

"Sleeping during high school history class, were you?" One eyebrow goes up in a superior way. "December seventh, 1941. Pearl Harbor? Ring a bell?"

It does, of course, but I didn't realize it mattered. "Well, duh. But big deal. That happened like, forever ago. I prefer to look forward. Not behind me."

"So you're condemned to repeat history, is that it?"

I scowl. I know one piece of history I'll never repeat, and it happened precisely the night of my first college frat party. "Believe it or not, every day on the calendar is the anniversary of something awful that happened in history. I mean, September eleventh, the Kennedy assassination, the Challenger explosion... If people went by that, they'd *never* be able to have any happy events in their lives."

"Yeah, but the bombing of Pearl Harbor's a pretty—"

"Do. Not. Speak. Okay?"

He shrugs. "All right."

That lasts until the end of the next song. After that, he scratches his almost-beard and says, "So...that maid of honor of yours...what's her name?"

"Eva." I sigh. I'm sure he's going to bring up how she assaulted him by touching his ski jacket. "What about her?"

"Just asking. She's hot. She got a guy?"

I can't help taking my eyes off the road and gawking at him. He thinks she's hot? Well, yes, obviously, she is. Eva is a tall, statuesque blonde who looks like she stepped off a magazine cover. Aaron's always saying how hot she is. But I've never actually heard Miles throw admiring comments at, well, anyone.

As much as I love Eva, I've had my share of green-with-envy moments. First of all, she comes from a fabulously wealthy family, and while she doesn't flaunt it, because we're so close, it always ends up right in my face. She travels all over the world on her vacations, and makes heads turn wherever she goes. People didn't notice me in high school, most of all, because they were blinded by *her* golden light.

And yes, she usually dates the hottest guys, so I suppose Miles would qualify. They'd probably make one of those enviable Hollywood power couples. Meva. Or Eviles?

When Eva came home from Yale that first winter break (did I mention she was absolutely brilliant, too?), and I introduced her to gorgeous Aaron, it was the first time I'd ever felt like I had something she didn't. I had the popular, hot, totally into-me boyfriend, and she was still searching the field of frat boy losers who weren't interested in steady relationships.

"No. She's single." I give him a sideways glance. "She told me how you nearly killed her for complimenting your ski jacket. So if you were trying to get her interest, you're making a good impression."

"Yeah?" He thinks I'm serious. "She touched me. You tell her not to touch me?"

"I did. She didn't listen. She likes to touch. Unlike you."

"I'd be okay with it, under the right circumstances."

I think about him flirting with her, especially since he never really flirted with me, and I get a sour feeling in my stomach. No. Flirting is beneath Miles. I know the way he gets women into bed. He plays the strong, silent type.

The second he opens his mouth, they go running.

"Do those *right circumstances* involve a massive vat of hand sanitizer?"

He ignores me, tapping his chin thoughtfully. "Huh."

I can't help being a little shocked. Aaron once told me the reason Miles is single is because he has hopelessly high expectations for women. According to Aaron, no one lives up to whatever his idea of the perfect woman is. He probably wants double D's, a model's face, and lord knows what else. Eva is stunningly gorgeous and might fulfill many of those expectations, but...

I'm floored. Has someone *real* actually penetrated Miles' bubble of perfection?

Well, besides me. But that was just one night. And a big, drunken mistake.

I really want to know what's going through his head, now. "So...wait. You like her?"

He laughs. "You should know by now. I don't like anyone. But exceptions can be made."

Right. Exceptions can be made. He'll let her touch him, just long enough to make him come.

Now I'm really feeling sick. "Seriously. Stay away from my friends. Trust me when I say this—none of them is right for you."

He cocks an eyebrow at me. "What do you mean, right for me? How do you know what's right for me?"

"I mean, not one of them is *batshit crazy*. Like you." I realize I'm laying off the gas and going fifty in a sixty-five when a truck moves around the dotted yellow line and barrels past me. I press on the gas with my flip-flop. "They want certain things from their men. Namely, someone who doesn't get grossed out every time she touches him."

"It depends on what kind of touching you're talking about."

Yes, I know he's not against all touching. Oh boy, do I know. My first night with him made that abundantly clear.

I do not need to be thinking about that! If there's ever a day that'll live in infamy, it's that one.

"Stop. Just…she's not interested. She'll never be interested. Let's leave it at that. Okay?"

He shrugs. "But who knows…with the alcohol properly flowing…the lights dimmed just the right amount…"

Oh, I definitely know how that can be.

We've been on the road for fifteen minutes and how are we supposed to make it for the other nine hours and forty-five?

Simple.

I have to tune him out. Get in the zone. Remember I'm marrying Aaron tomorrow, and everything's going to be rainbows and sunshine. I'm going to have the best day of my life.

I must ignore Miles Foster.

So I mutter, "I know. It has a way of making people make the biggest mistakes of their lives."

And look at that. I've effectively shut him up.

2:26 PM, DECEMBER 6

Miles and I are actually very good at pretending the other doesn't exist.

That's because, despite our passionate hate for one another, we were often thrust together, due to having Aaron in common.

It was never comfortable, but we dealt with it.

And the weird thing is, when the three of us are together, Aaron'll always mention it to us like it's some big joke, because to him, it's funny as hell. Aaron's big on bringing up the past, especially the stupid drunken escapades of his college glory days, because he's King where stupid drunken escapades are concerned. "Hey. Remember that time, before Lia and I got together? How you two…"

Yeah. Funny. *Hilarious.*

Usually, when that happens, Miles and I will do everything possible to pretend the other doesn't exist.

Then I will politely remind Aaron how drunk we all were. After all, the reason it happened in the first place was because Aaron had gone off to get me that beer, and then never returned. He got caught up doing naked keg stands and passed out, as he tells it, "On the bar with my dick hanging out!"

According to local Delta Phi legend, Aaron was big on passing out naked with his dick hanging out. It seems that every brother can relate a different story about it. Just like no brother can relate a story about Miles having a good time at one of their keggers.

After the moment passes, one of us will make a comment like, "Whew! Good thing we've all moved past that train wreck of a night!"

And we have. Totally.

So, with an imaginary brick wall between us, we make excellent time going over the mountain range that lies between Boulder and the Midnight Lodge.

After our initial conversation, we don't talk. Not once.

I listen to my favorite country station until I lose a signal, and then I pipe in my playlist, which alternates between country and pop. Miles puts his earbuds in and listens to whatever he likes to listen to…probably a bunch of old men disagreeing with one another. When we come down the mountain, I'm happy.

The sky is still clear, the sun is shining, I'm getting married in the morning, and Miles has effectively been beaten into silence.

Life is good.

I have to get gas in my Mini before we head back, so I pull into the Shell and stop at the gas pump. I reach down at his feet and grab my purse. The second I do, he pops out his earbuds.

"Allow me."

He climbs out of the car. At first I think he's being chivalrous, but then I see him reaching his arms over his head and rolling his shoulder joints. He's just wanting to stretch, since he's been folded up inside my car for too long.

I watch him in the driver's side mirror as he lifts his arms to the sky, lifting his shirt just enough to bare about three inches of his rock-hard abs. I find my mind wandering down a dangerous path as I realize he's walking toward me.

Like a moron, I squeeze my eyes closed.

Suddenly, there's a slight tapping on the glass.

I look up and see him peering at me. "Eighty-nine okay?"

For the briefest moment, I flash to his museum-like room, lying on top of him in sixty-nine.

Yeah, believe it or not, Mr. Clean and I went at it like fucking rabbits that night, in a bunch of positions I'd never even known *existed*. By morning we were both sweaty and dirty and—

What the fuck am I doing?

My temperature skyrockets until I blink the image away. *You moron. He's asking about the gas.*

"Ninety-one, please." I reach into my purse and filter my Mastercard through the two-inch opening in the window.

He shakes his head. "Forget it. Early wedding gift, from me to you."

Nice, but if you wanted to give me something I really could use, how about a lobotomy?

Trying not to watch as he fills up my tank, I grab my phone and look at my texts. The first one I see is from Eva: *I heard you went with the asshole. Poor you.*

I type in: *Yep. Just got here. Be back in 5 hours.*

I look at the clock. It's just after two-thirty, so if we zip over to Aaron's apartment, get the rings and don't stop, we'll be back at the Midnight Lodge by seven-thirty, which will give me enough time to slip into my dress for the rehearsal dinner. Perfect.

By then, Aaron should be sober. And ready. I try not to be a total nudge when it comes to him having fun, because I know how much he likes it, but if he insists on going out with his buddies tonight, after the rehearsal dinner, I'll have to put my foot down. *Last* night was the last hurrah. He doesn't need another one. And the Guppy can avoid drinking like a fish for one night.

Although, I know how he gets when all of his friends and frat brothers are around. Most of them are scattered around the country, now. He rarely has time to be with all of them together, so on an occasion like this...

I realize I'm gnawing on my lip again, thinking about what happened the *last* time he and his brothers all got together, nineteen months ago, for a D-Phi Almost-Graduation shebang.

It was bad.

Really, really bad.

So bad, I don't want to think about it.

So I type in: *Have you seen Aaron yet?*

A moment later: *Yep. He and the rest of the groomsmen have taken ownership of the restaurant. They're eating everything in sight.*

Hmm. Nice that Aaron doesn't have to worry about fitting into his tux the way I have to worry about fitting into my dress.

I exit out of the message to her and look for a text from Aaron, but there isn't one.

Of course not. When he's with his friends, he reverts back to his frat boy self. Meaning that he forgets about me.

Which really worries me.

West wouldn't put up with this shit. He's never said as much, but I can tell he thinks his soon-to-be brother-in-law is a bit of a jerk. Which is why he didn't go to the bachelor party. West wasn't one for wild parties and drunken antics, even when he was in college. And though he goes through women like Kleenex, he's a good big brother. One of my favorite people. He's all about defending my honor.

Plus, his was the shoulder I cried on, right before college graduation, when I thought that Aaron and I were over.

I sigh as I hear the click at the pump, signaling my tank is full. Miles lifts the nozzle and puts it back in place, then takes the receipt and opens the door as I'm typing in a text to West.

West, could you please keep an eye on Aaron? Make sure he doesn't

When I look up, I realize Miles is watching me. I can't see his eyes through the sunglasses, but I get the feeling he knows exactly what I'm up to. Fucking Dumbledore.

My eyes trail back to the text. *Make sure he doesn't* what, exactly? How possessive and stupid do I look? I'm marrying Aaron. He's the man I trust with my heart.

At least, I should.

No, I do. That's why we're getting married.

He proved to me he was a changed man. Sure, we'd had a bumpy road before graduation, but it's been smooth sailing ever since he proposed.

Delete, delete, delete.

I shove my phone into my bag. "Let's be off!" I say brightly.

He grunts.

It's funny. Whenever Miles is in a bad mood, it somehow puts me in a good mood. It's like we're absolute opposites in that respect. If that isn't pure hate, I don't know what is.

"Thanks for the gas, buddy!" I say, backing out of my spot at the pump. I resist the urge to give his big, flannel-clad biceps a friendly punch. "Now let's get moving and get those rings, Samwise!"

He cocks an eye at me. "Samwise?"

"Yeah. Of course, I'm Frodo."

"So…what? Is Aaron Gollum?"

I roll my eyes. "Oh, whatever. Of course it's not a perfect analogy, but I'm permitted to take liberties. I'm getting married tomorrow!"

"Uh-huh," he says, burying his nose in his phone. "On to Mordor."

2:45 PM, DECEMBER 6

The apartment Aaron has in Boulder is right across from the fire station, and about a block from the CU Boulder campus. It's also within walking distance of the D-Phi frat house. Though we graduated nineteen months ago, he's still guest of honor at their parties. He was on the seven-year plan and wound up graduating the same time I did, even though he's three years older than I am.

What can I say? Even though he's not in college anymore, he couldn't fully detach himself from that world. He still considers it the best time of his life, which is probably why he's constantly bringing up those old stories.

Aaron's had it pretty good, though, since graduating with his degree in electrical engineering. His father is CEO of an engineering firm in downtown Boulder, so he got him a great job there. We think he can make manager in another couple years, if he keeps at it. He's been trying to put away money so that we can buy a house.

Me? Well, I'm another story. I graduated with a degree in English and couldn't find a job anywhere. I blanketed the world with resumes, and nothing came of it. So I decided to go back for my Masters in Library Science and add to my already impressive student loan debt. I'm still living in the same apartment that I had for my undergrad, but the lease runs out at the first of the year. When we're married, I'll move in with Aaron.

That's the plan.

I can't wait. My apartment on campus is just a dorm. But sharing his place with him, starting our lives together as man and wife? Maybe it'll feel like a home.

Next to me, Miles is drumming his hands on his thighs, something I've noticed he only does when he's nervous.

Hmm. I wonder what that's about?

Miles may be Aaron's best friend, but he didn't get into D-Phi the way Aaron did. He *easily* transitioned off campus. He graduated summa cum laude from CU in the usual four years with a dual degree in business and math and cut all ties with D-Phi and everything college. Then, he got a job as an investments manager at some big-deal firm in Denver, where he quickly climbed the ranks and is now vice president. He's rolling, though you wouldn't know to look at him most days, since he seems to favor the Paul Bunyan look over suits and ties. Aaron's always saying what a "lucky son of a bitch" Miles is, but I think it's a lot more than luck.

First of all, he's a genius.

I'm not just saying that.

Oh, you know that beer pong he was watching the first night I saw him? He wasn't staring dumbly into space, stoned. I learned later, when I saw all the napkins he had scattered around him, that he was working out a formula to find the exact trajectory and velocity or something—I wasn't paying attention when he explained it—so that one of his brothers could hit a cup, every single time. And he'd been testing it with Aaron, which was why he was cleaning up against all the poor, unsuspecting girls who happened to challenge him.

Somewhere, in the drunken haze, I remember asking him why he didn't play beer pong, testing out his own theories himself, and he'd actually said, "Because it doesn't sufficiently interest me."

I'd asked him what did, and he'd said, "You," right before he kissed me.

My heart flutters a little at the thought, but I clamp a hand over it to remind it to chill out.

Wrong guy. Wrong, wrong, *really fucking wrong* guy.

As I pull into the parking lot of the Grammercy Acres, Aaron's apartment building, I swallow a few times, trying to rid myself of the memory of Miles' taste. Drunk as I was, I've somehow managed to keep so many memories of that night not only intact, but absolutely crystalline-clear. It's a curse, I'm sure. Meanwhile, Miles probably doesn't remember a damn thing.

I coast into Aaron's spot outside the building, cut the engine, and hold my hand out to Miles.

But he's already reaching for the door. As he slips out, he says, "I'll get them. You stay here."

"What? No." I open my door and jump out, following him up the narrow pathway.

Halfway up the sidewalk, he wheels on me. He wags a finger in my direction. "What are you doing? Just go back to the car."

I cross my arms, standing toe to toe with him, doing my best to stare him down even though he's a foot taller than I am. "No. I want to make sure he didn't forget anything else. Besides, I have to use the bathroom. I haven't peed in five hours."

He lets out a long breath. "Fine. Whatever."

He heads to the apartment, walking fast, and I nearly trip over myself trying to keep up. Damn his long legs. When I get to the door, he's already opened it and gone through, leaving it just barely cracked for me.

I push the door open and look around. Yep, it's just the same as it was the day before he left, when I stopped by before we all caravanned it over the mountain. There's clothing strewn everywhere from his whirlwind packing expedition. His giant red sectional is barely visible, it's so covered in shit.

As I'm crossing to the bedroom, Miles appears in the door, holding a velvet bag. "Your rings."

I take them from him and peek inside. There they are. A little thrill passes through me as I touch the cool platinum. The tension I've felt in my neck this whole trip starts to ease.

"Geez, this place is a shithole."

I raise my head to see Miles' eyes ping-ponging around the place, that superior glare back. I've never been to his flat in downtown Denver, but I imagine that his housekeeping staff must hate working for him.

But he's right. It's a bachelor pad. There's not a painting on the wall or a decorative element anywhere. "So he's not Martha Stewart. I'll fix things when I move in."

"Will you?" He seems doubtful.

Well, I'm sure nothing I ever do will be up to his standards. Sometimes I'm surprised I even made him come as many times as he did.

Ugh, why am I thinking of that?

I hand him the rings. "You should take these, then. You're not going to lose them, are you?"

He takes the bag, opens the flap on his flannel shirt pocket, and tucks them in. "No."

It's sad that even though I hate him, I trust him. Miles is a man of his word. He promises, he delivers. Aaron should have entrusted the rings to him to begin with; then maybe none of this would've ever happened.

Stepping through the minefield of discarded crap on the shag rug, I head toward the bathroom door, which is right across the narrow hallway from Aaron's bedroom.

Suddenly, Miles says, his voice an octave higher than usual, "Wait. Where you going?"

I point to the bathroom. "I told you."

"Oh. Right." Relaxing, he thrusts his hands into his pockets and strolls around the living room, taking it all in. He kicks one of Aaron's sneakers with the toe of his boot and shakes his head.

Aw, Mr. Clean is about to blow a gasket.

As I walk toward the bathroom, though, I get a distinctly odd feeling. It only grows as I yank my leggings over my thighs, sit down on the toilet and pee.

Aaron insisting Miles come with me.

Miles fidgeting when I pulled up at the apartment and trying to get me to stay in the car.

Miles being nervous when I walked toward the bedroom.

As I'm finishing up, looking for some soap and a towel so I can wash and dry my hands, it hits me.

There's something in Aaron's bedroom that he doesn't want me to see.

I dry my hands on my leggings since I can't find a towel, telling myself I'm being stupid. Aaron sent Miles along with me because he didn't want me going alone. He cares about me. That's all there is to it. And Miles was acting nervous and weird because, well, Miles *is* weird.

Still, by the time I'm ready to open the door, I know I will not be able to leave unless I know for sure.

Taking a deep breath, I crack open the door to the hallway. Not seeing Miles, I step across the hall as quietly as possible and push open the door to his bedroom.

I don't know what I'm expecting to find. A naked woman sleeping there? Long blonde hairs all over the bed? The last time I'd slept here—in fact, the last time we slept together—was nearly two months ago. I suggested—and Aaron agreed—that our wedding night would be much more exciting if we hadn't gotten any in a while.

I find everything as I expected. White, unpainted walls, scuffed in places, except for a giant framed painting of the Boulder Flatirons at the head of his bed. I'd given it to him a month ago, for his birthday. I'd gotten it from a local artist's gallery as the start of a promise—that when I moved in, I'd make this place homey and livable. I'd make it *ours*, not just four walls and a roof.

Other than that, his king bed, sheets all rumpled in a pile at the very center. His dresser, all but one drawer open and vomiting clothes.

Nothing else.

But then my eyes settle on the night table drawer. I've never looked in there before, but it must be where he keeps important things, since he kept the rings there.

I hurry over to it and yank it open.

The first thing my eyes fall on is a dog-eared picture of us, at the D-Phi semi-formal, taken years ago. It's my favorite picture; I actually have a copy of it blown up and framed in my apartment. I sit down on the bed, lifting and admiring it. We're so young there.

My eyes fall back to the drawer...and the yellow box of condoms.

I tamp down the initial urge to freak out. Sure, I've been on the pill forever, and we stopped using condoms four years ago. They could just be old. And Aaron's a pack-rat. He never throws anything away.

Even though he only moved here a year and a half ago...there's got to be an explanation.

I lift it out, looking for the expiration date.

As I do, I notice the half-used tube of lube.

Half-used...and I know he's never used it with *me*. He's always trying to get in my back door, but I've been pretty firmly closed for business on that front. I mean, really. What is the allure of anal, anyway?

Don't guys use lube to masturbate? So, that's probably not a big deal. But *that,* and the condoms, and the fact that Aaron clearly didn't want me snooping in here...

I look up suddenly as Miles' form fills the doorway.

He's gazing at me, and at the condoms and lube in my lap, with an expression I can't read.

Then he says, "Are you ready?"

I replace the contents quickly and stand up. "Um, yeah."

As I follow him out the door, I can't breathe. Because I thought I'd resolved this with Aaron. And now there are all these doubts. Less than twenty hours before I'm supposed to marry him.

I need air.

I need to talk to Eva.

I need Xanax.

I most definitely do not need the six feet three inches of sarcastic man-flesh that I'm doomed to spend the next five hours with. Aaron's partner in crime, who I think may have actually been working in cahoots with Aaron to keep this from me.

I walk through the apartment behind Miles, in a daze, and part of me wants to punch him.

He goes to open the door, but I attack it, slamming it closed. "Is that why you came here?"

He looks annoyed. "What?"

"I mean, the condoms, the lube…we never use any of that, and—"

"Huh? Get out of the way, Shorty, or you're gonna—"

He's deflecting. I won't have it. "No. You know what I'm talking about. Did Aaron make you come here because he wanted you to keep things from me?"

He glares down at me for a long moment. I brace myself for the news. I can already almost feel it, harder than a smack across the face.

But it doesn't come.

He easily nudges me out of the way and opens the door. "Your upcoming nuptials are making you into even more of a headcase than usual."

He goes through the door and down the steps, leaving me alone.

Miles is right.

I *am* being a headcase.

But this is the rest of my life I'm talking about. And…

I step outside and pull the door shut as he's reaching the bottom of the stairs.

"Miles!" I cry desperately.

He stops on the last step and turns to look up at me as he puts on his mirrored sunglasses.

"Please. You would tell me, right? If he was..." I can't bring myself to say the word. "You know. Right?"

His mouth stays a straight line. I know what that means.

I'm Aaron's friend. Not yours. Don't ask me these questions.

He shoves his hands into his pockets, tilts his head to the sky, and lets out a breath. "Want me to drive?"

I swallow and follow him down the steps. No, he wouldn't tell me. He's loyal to one person only: Aaron. His best friend. His only friend. "No. I'll drive."

I didn't notice the clouds coming in, or the air getting colder. When I reach the car, an arctic blast of wind rips across the parking lot, making my teeth chatter and my bare toes curl. I rip open the door and slide into the warmth of the car.

And as if I couldn't feel any worse, the second I start the engine, the first tiny snowflakes scatter across the windshield.

3:06 PM, DECEMBER 6

I am not *that* much of a headcase.

Okay, yes, I am a little paranoid. I am a little possessive. And I'm a little neurotic.

But I swear, I wasn't any of those things until nineteen months ago.

That's another date that will live in infamy. April fourteenth.

It was my senior year in college, and I was a month away from graduating with my English degree. I'd been sending out resumes and getting zero response. I had exams and papers out the wazoo. I'd just gotten a letter saying how much my undergrad monthly student loan payments were going to be.

Life was pretty much in the crapper.

The only good thing I had going on was Aaron. We'd weathered nearly four years together, and so he was a constant in my life. And it was pretty great. Sure, we had a few little rough patches where we'd break up, but we always got back together within the week. I'd spend nearly every weekend night at the frat house, and I always had a party to go to, so I was crazy popular as Aaron's girlfriend. I barely remembered what life had been like before him, when I was that scared little wallflower nobody.

He'd only had two classes that last semester, so he'd been living the high life, really enjoying his last year as an undergrad. While I was always nose to the grindstone with English papers, he was constantly in the basement of his frat house, drinking and playing darts.

So there was an entire week when I was studying for my Chaucer final that I hardly saw Aaron at all. I missed him like crazy, thought about him every spare moment, but I had to turn down all the invitations to end-of-year parties, because I'd bombed the midterm and really needed to get an A on the final to make Dean's List.

The minute I finished, though, I was so excited and relieved that I didn't even stop at my apartment. I went straight to the frat house.

I remember walking down the plush red carpet, toward Aaron's room, ready to throw myself into his arms.

Miles had graduated three years prior, but maybe if he'd been there, he'd have poked his head out and tried to cover for his best friend. But Aaron was Miles-less. And it turned out to be his downfall.

I opened the door and found him lying on his back in bed, some naked blonde bouncing on his cock, in midst of a monster-sized orgasm. It's amazing I didn't hear her outside the door, considering how loudly she was screaming.

Two things occurred to me. One: that Aaron never looked that excited when I was on top of him; and two: she had way bigger boobs than I had.

And just like that, everything good in my life went poof.

I whirled around and went back the way I came, still numb with disbelief.

There had to be some mistake. He'd called me just a couple hours ago to wish me good luck on my exam. He told me he still had a hangover from the previous night's party, so he was going to turn in early. I didn't realize that he was going to bring company.

Seconds later, I heard his footsteps behind me. He caught me on the mansion's massive mahogany staircase, the one that leads down to the foyer with stained-glass windows too pretty for a frat house. He grabbed my arm. "Lia."

That's all he could say. He didn't need to say more. It was definitely what it looked like. He couldn't back out of it with some lame excuse.

Still, I didn't want to believe. So I said the stupidest thing. I said, "Are you cheating on me?"

He glanced over the railing, where a bunch of his brothers were all standing, watching the whole sordid exchange with smirks of amusement on their faces.

He was wearing boxers, and his cock was still hard, making a little tent in front of him. In a minute's time, he'd gone from my everything to someone I didn't know. He said, "She's no one. I just missed you."

"Well, I'm here," I'd murmured. But right then, I wanted to be anywhere else. "I think I'll just go."

I'd walked awkwardly away, and this time, he didn't stop me. I remember thinking that was it. I was devastated without Aaron. I felt as if I might as well lie down and die.

I have no idea what Aaron did after that. Maybe he went and finished off with the girl. But about an hour later, the texts started. He sent me about a thousand of them. At first I refused to answer. Gradually, I softened. By graduation, we were talking again, and I was considering giving him another chance, despite West's assertions that I could do better.

When he dropped to his knee and proposed as soon as I left the stage with my diploma, well…that was that.

He didn't flash a ring and make me crumble. No, he knelt down and took my hands in his, like he was worshiping me. He gave this long speech about how he'd changed. How it took this "dark period" in our relationship to show him exactly what I meant to him. How he was nothing without me.

Aaron knew how to go big or go home. And he liked the audience, which we had. Over a thousand people watched, waiting for my answer.

So by the time I said yes, I was sobbing.

And after we'd gone shopping and found the ring, and he'd slipped the ring on my finger, it felt like night and day.

Post-College Aaron was attentive. Post-College Aaron didn't visit the frat house every day, or drink heavily, or meet with his friends and act like a goofball. Post-College Aaron didn't care about being the life of the party. Oh, he talked about those things, but he really put in the effort to get all that behind him.

He'd turned himself around. The closer the wedding got, the more reassured I was that I'd made the right decision.

Which was why, after about nine months, I told him he should go to D-Phi for alumni events or to hang with his friends. I knew he wanted to, and I didn't want to be that drill sergeant wife and have too tight a leash on him.

But now, I don't know.

I don't know anything.

I'm probably just overreacting. At least, I hope I am.

My hands are wrapped so tightly around the steering wheel that they're shaking, and it has nothing to do with the snow that's steadily falling as we approach the mountains.

Miles doesn't know that. He says, "You sure you don't want me to drive?"

"I'm good." I turn up the radio and try to get into a Carrie Underwood song.

Despite what he thinks, my Mini Cooper is not all that awful in snow. It has always handled pretty well. And though I really can't stand the white fluffy stuff, I don't have much of a problem driving in it. The only problem I have is with the weather app on my phone. The one that said this shit wasn't going to arrive until tonight.

The snowflakes are big and wet, so I turn on the headlights and the windshield wipers. Luckily, there are very few cars on the road at this time on a Friday afternoon, so if we keep at this clip, we should still be able to make it, no problem.

All's okay. This wedding will be great. So what if the snow is a little early? So what if Aaron's acting suspiciously? So FUCKING WHAT?

"Hey." Miles snaps his fingers at me. "Chill out."

I stare straight ahead. "What are you talking about? I am chilled out," I retort.

"Right. Sure you don't want me to drive?"

That's when I realize we're climbing the hill, and I'm only doing thirty. No wonder there's a pickup with its grill up my ass.

I sigh. There's a turnout before we get to the real high hairpin turns. "All right."

Flipping on my blinker, I pull over to the side of the road. When I stop, Miles unlatches his seat belt. I watch the snow falling, and falling, and FUCKING FALLING, and somehow I get the feeling maybe *that's* God, trying to tell me something.

I freak out.

I drop my head to the steering wheel.

Miles says and does absolutely nothing. Jason Aldean croons and the wind whistles outside, shaking the car a little.

"You know he cheated on me," I say, more to the steering wheel than to him. "Don't you?"

I turn to look at him. He nods, his mouth a straight line. "Yeah. He told me."

He told him. Really? It makes me wonder what *else* he told him.

What else Miles could tell *me*. Things that I'd really, *really* like to know before entering into a lifelong commitment with his best friend.

I take a deep breath. "And I know that you and I hate each other. But I hope that because I'm Aaron's girlfriend and we're a package deal, and you care about Aaron, you'd also, by default, care about me?"

His voice is casual. "Uh. Sure."

I'm not sure I believe that, but I forge ahead anyway, because I'm feeling desperate.

"So even though you hate me, if you saw me getting myself into a bad situation, you'd put the brakes on it, right?"

Understanding begins to trickle in. His voice is hard, but he flicks his eyes away for a second. Like he doesn't want me to see something there. As if the guy's even readable. "You know what you're getting into."

"But what if I don't? What if I'm being blind?" I cry, glancing at the clock in the dashboard. We've got to go. Time is ticking and it's starting to snow harder. "Look. I love Aaron.

I love him more than I've ever loved anyone. But if he can't keep it in his pants and I'm in for sixty more years of this shit, I want to know going in."

He studies me closely, and at first I think he's going to call me a headcase again. "Would it matter?"

I blink. How could he think something like that wouldn't matter? "What?"

"You heard me."

I let out a laugh. "Of course. You think it wouldn't matter to me?"

He nods slowly. "What I mean is, you have five hundred of your closest friends and family on the other side of this mountain range, waiting for the wedding of the century. You've been planning it for the better part of two years and have socked all of your daddy's money into it. Say you find out that Aaron's been cheating on you since Day One. Do you really mean to tell me you'd just call it off? Just like that?"

I stare at him. "Well, I…yes?"

My voice is weak with indecision.

He's right. I'm so far into this, I hardly even feel there's a choice anymore, even if…

Oh, god.

"Here's the deal. Aaron texted me and told me to go with you and get the rings. That's all. I have no idea why he wanted me to go in and get them. Maybe because he wanted me to protect you, or maybe because he knew you'd go all psycho if you saw the lube. I don't know. I just did as he said. All right?"

I hang my head, speechless.

"And I also think the two of you have made your bed and are already drifting off to sleep in it. You made your choice.

The invitations are out. The guests have arrived. Get it?" He shrugs. "So, that's why, even if I *did* know something about Aaron's extracurricular activities not involving you—which I'm not saying I do—I wouldn't be telling you. It. Doesn't. Matter."

The radio cuts to a mattress commercial with an annoying jingle. Outside, the snow pelting the car sounds more like hail. The car rocks back and forth on another gust of wind.

Of course, once again, Dumbledore has a point. God, I hate him.

"So get your ass up and let's switch already," he mutters.

Right. I open the door a crack, but then the wind takes it and makes it fly wide open. Before I step out, I realize how serious things are getting.

There are already a couple inches on the ground. The biting wind goes right through my leggings. Hugging my hoodie closed, I slip in my less-than-adequate flip-flops and nearly end up sliding onto my butt twice by the time I'm in the passenger's seat.

By then, I'm an icicle. I turn up the heat and direct the vents toward my face.

God of Snow that Miles is, he takes his time, sauntering through the weather, and opens the door and slides inside in a leisurely way.

"Close the door, for god's sake!" I shriek at him.

He does, pulling off his skullcap and shaking it. Now his hair is all staticky and his cheeks are red. It's a good look on him. Me? I probably look as miserable as I feel.

He gives me a once-over and smirks. "Flip-flops. You're a piece of work, Bridezilla."

I press my lips together, willing myself to build that little wall between us and find a happy place.

"And guess what?" He grabs the handle under him and shoves the driver's seat all the way back. "I think you're going to have the S-word for your wedding."

I don't say anything, because I think Dumbledore may be right.

Again.

3:35 PM, DECEMBER 6

My phone has never been the greatest at holding a charge. I should probably be conserving its life, considering I left my charging cable at the resort and I'm only at fifty percent.

But I can't help it. The snow keeps falling, and I'm freaking out.

I punch in a call to the man who's always had my back. My big brother, West.

West is a bit of an oddball himself, though no one can be as odd as Miles. West, like Miles, likes to do his own thing and never lets anyone tell him anything. But West works in L.A. for one of the movie studios. He's one of the youngest and most successful producers in the city. He's surrounded by phonies all the time, which he hates. But my brother is seriously the realest and most honest person I've ever known.

I adore him beyond all comprehension. He always talks me down from the ledge.

"Why the hell didn't you send me, Dahl?" he asks before I can even say hello. "I would've gone for you."

I know he would've. He's so gold-hearted. "I didn't want to bother you. And I didn't know where you were."

"Ah, shit, Dahl. You know you've got Mom climbing the walls. Dad's about to have a heart attack."

I cringe. That's the last thing I want to hear. "Well. We're making pretty good time. I'm still shooting to be there for the rehearsal."

"All right. But don't take any chances. I want you back here in one piece."

I look over at Miles, who is starting to drum his hands on the steering wheel. And no wonder. There's a car in front of us going no more than twenty miles per hour, and we're in a no-passing zone.

I cover the mouthpiece and whisper, "Blow the horn!"

Miles gives me a disgusted look. "No."

"This is just a freaking dusting!" I shout, as if the person driving the old boat of a Volvo ahead of us can hear.

Miles puts his elbow against the door and leans on it, frustrated. Partly at the car in front of us, but probably mostly at me.

I go back to my phone conversation. "So have you seen Aaron?" I ask hopefully, reaching over and trying to press on the horn.

Miles swats me away before I can get there. "Don't touch my wheel."

"Yeah. He's worried about you, obviously. We all are. We want you back," West says, and I smile. "But I'm sorry, Dahl. That was a prick move. Forgetting the rings and then making you go back for them? I almost kicked his ass."

I frown. My brother and Aaron are definitely on some shaky ground. They're pretty different. "Don't blame him. I was the one who wanted to go back for the rings. He told me not to."

"He was the bonehead who left them behind to begin with. After all your planning. Shit, Dahl." He sounds frustrated, like he wants to say more but he bites it back with a hard clench of his jaw.

God, but even when he says little, he knows *just* what to say. He's one of the few people who gets how insane this wedding planning has made me, and how much work has gone into it. Aaron doesn't. But to spend nearly two years of my life making every detail perfect, and not to be recognized for it...it stings. "Thanks, West. But it'll still be fine. I know it. It'll all work out."

"Yeah. I mean, Aaron and I might not see eye to eye, but I know how you feel about him. And I want you to be happy. I want you to have the day of your dreams, Peanut."

I laugh. He hasn't called me that in years. "It will be. You'll see."

I tell him goodbye and hang up, feeling so much more relaxed.

But the second I do, Miles pulls his foot off the gas so we're going less than twenty miles per hour.

What. The. Fuck? We're never going to get there if we go fifteen miles per hour the whole way.

Before I can reach for the horn again, I see the red tail lights of a line of traffic, stopped up ahead.

Exasperated, I reach over and manage to get closer to the horn this time, but he drapes his broad chest over the wheel. "I don't care if you're getting married tomorrow," he warns. "I will break your fingers if you touch this steering wheel while I'm driving again."

Shooting him my fiercest scowl but properly scolded, I slump back in the chair like a sullen child.

I guess he's right. The traffic is nearly stopped, cars as far as the eye can see. Blowing the horn won't do any good.

4:30 PM, DECEMBER 6

This is a big problem.

We've been in a non-moving line of cars for about forty minutes.

Darkness is falling fast. Everything is a dismal gray. I can barely see up ahead, with all the snow blowing around. Red taillights, stretching out into oblivion, are occasionally visible in the whiteout.

Miles drops his hand onto the brake, wrapping his big fingers around the knob. He rolled up the sleeves of his flannel as he drove, probably because I'm blasting the heat, since my toes are ice cubes. His forearm is veined and masculine and threatens to flash me back to the rest of his perfect body parts. They might be covered, but I have intimate knowledge of them, and having them this close is seriously a recipe for disaster.

Why did I ever think this was a good idea?

Oh, right. I never did.

I should've done this alone.

Or maybe I shouldn't have done it at all. Why was I so insistent that everything be absolutely perfect?

Cars have been steadily coming down the hill. But going up isn't happening. Next to me, Miles cranes his neck again to try to see what's going on. "Why didn't we stop to get something to eat, again? I'm starving."

"Because we hate each other and don't want to spend any more time together than absolutely necessary," I mutter, my foot up on the dash as I try to lacquer my little toenail. "Quit moving."

"It's the wind, dumbass."

I know that. It still feels better to yell at him. Even though we haven't moved in the better part of an hour, I can't keep my hand straight because of the way the wind's bouncing the car around.

This is what I've been reduced to. Where today I could've gotten the whole-body treatment, now, I'm forced to take desperate measures. Which means, giving myself a shabby little pedicure in the passenger seat of my Mini. I had a dull file and some lavender nail polish, which is better than nothing. Tomorrow, I can wake extra early and get everything taken care of so I'm perfect for go-time.

I'm trying to ignore the fact that even if we did the speed limit the whole way to the Midnight Lodge, we'd still end up there a half-hour late for the rehearsal dinner.

As I finish with my pinky toe, my phone lights up with another text from Eva: *Oh god. This is awful!*

I text back: *It's okay. It's just a squall. It should end soon.*

Then I get a text from Aaron: *Hurry back soon, babe. I'll be ready. Can't wait for tomorrow.*

I smile as I blow on my toenails. What was I so worried about, again?

Then I look at the next text that came in from Eva: *Sorry to break it to you, but your mom was just watching The Weath-*

er Channel in her room and says that the snow isn't supposed to stop until tomorrow morning.

What? I almost spill the little vial of nail polish I have on the center console, rushing to flip the radio station. I whirl the dial, not coming up with anything. "Can you find that station you listen to? Boredom 105? I need to hear the weather."

He snorts. "Forget it. We're out of range for all the Denver stations."

I grab my phone and check the weather. Sure enough, for the town we're in—someplace called, aptly, Desperation—it shows snow until seven in the morning. There's also a blizzard warning in effect until six AM.

Oh, fuck.

Making plans to write a strongly worded letter to every weatherman in the metropolitan area, I throw my head back and groan. As I do, a sharp gust of wind rocks the car, sending a jolt of fear down my spine. Have cars ever been picked up on this mountain and sent airborne into the ravine? Specifically, little cars?

I hope not.

When the wind calms, I bang my fist on the armrest. "What the fuck! Move already!! Did you hear me?!"

Miles just looks at me. "Hey. Headcase."

I pout. "It appears that it's a little more than a squall."

"You don't say."

Yes. Actually, I didn't say. *He* was the one who'd been saying that. Memo to me: When the guy you're traveling with is a genius and a wizard and has a history of never being wrong, *listen to him.*

Chicken wire sure is looking good, right now.

Hope dares to bloom inside me when the cars in front of us start to move.

Yes. Yes. Yes. *Keep it going.*

I wince when they suddenly stop. I should've known it was too good to be true. So we've gone about twenty feet in sixty minutes. At this rate, we'll get to the Midnight Lodge when I'm in dentures.

My toenails are now dry. They look awful, but they're better than before. I start to file my fingernails. I keep them short because of my biting habit. At least they're not bitten down to the quick and bloody, per usual. I've actually resorted to sleeping with bags on my hands lately because I sometimes bite them when I'm sleeping, and I wanted them to look good for the wedding.

But like Miles says, they're still awful.

As I'm filing away, red and blue lights appear in the rear-view mirror. A police car's driving up the shoulder, followed by an ambulance.

"Accident," I sigh, saying a quick prayer for whoever might've been hurt.

Miles drags a hand down his face and yawns. "Well, if they get it cleared out, we should be able to keep going."

"You think?" I check my phone. If we could perhaps go over the speed limit, maybe we won't be all that late.

"I don't know."

"If we can get clear, and you gun it all the way there, we might not be that late for the rehearsal."

He gives me a skeptical look. "Seriously?"

I nod.

"So let me ask you a question. Do you know how weddings work?"

I nod.

"Have you imagined your wedding since you were a little girl?"

"Well, yes."

"Do you know how to walk straight and say the words *I do*?"

Now, I know where he's headed with this. "Yes, but—"

"Then why the *fuck* do you need to rehearse any of that?"

I grip the nail file like a weapon, aimed at him. "Well, obviously, because I need to know where to stand and how to proceed in and all that."

"So, you'd rather us die on this mountain trying to get to your rehearsal than accidentally stand in the wrong place at the altar tomorrow?" He scratches his temple. "Makes perfect sense to me."

I hate him. I really do. But I laugh for some reason—maybe to hide the fact that he pushes my buttons far more than I'm comfortable with. "You're stupid. Besides, there's not going to be an altar tomorrow, dummy. It's a secular ceremony. And it's my once-in-a-lifetime, so it has to be perfect."

He laughs as the fleet of emergency vehicles passes us and disappears up ahead, beyond the curve in the road.

"Right. Too bad. Because if I were you, right now, I'd be praying that we get over this hill tonight."

My heart does a nervous little flip, though obviously, I *am* praying. "What do you mean? You just said it should be okay once we get past the accident."

"I was trying to keep you from stabbing me with that weapon of yours," he growls, staring straight ahead.

The cars ahead of us begin to move. We climb a little way up the mountain. In the lane with the opposing traffic, many cars start to pass by us. I hope that means that they've cleared whatever accident is up ahead. I start to applaud when we actually get over ten miles per hour.

But when we get around the mountain, my stomach drops.

All of those cars that are reaching the flashing lights? A police officer is directing them to turn around and head back down the mountain.

I'd started to paint my fingernails, but now I'm curling my hands into fists, smudging the polish something awful. "No," I whine. "No, no, no!"

"Relax," Miles mutters. "And put the fucking file down before you hurt someone."

I'm gripping it so hard I'm surprised it doesn't become a permanent part of my body. I loosen my grip. "Do you think I'm ridiculous? Because I didn't want chicken wire?"

"Chicken wire?"

"Yes. Aaron said I shouldn't go back for the rings because it was only a symbol. He said we could use chicken wire. But I wanted things to be perfect, and..." I cover my face with my hands. "I'm an idiot."

"You can't use chicken wire," he mumbles.

I twist my head to look at him, stunned. Is he actually, for once in his life...agreeing with me?

"But I never would've been so fucking stupid as hell to leave my wedding rings at home. Not if it meant that much to me."

I stiffen my shoulders, because his words are like an ice pick to the heart. "What are you insinuating? That Aaron's marrying me doesn't mean anything to him?"

He shrugs. "No. Just that he and I are different."

Right. I know that. Those differences are why I love Aaron, and I hate the man next to me.

But I hate admitting that Miles is right. He *never* would've forgotten the rings in the first place.

An officer is standing in the middle of the road, directing traffic. Miles pulls the car up to the officer and powers down the window. His tone of voice changes; he speaks to the officer like he's an actual human. "Hi, any chance we can get through?"

The officer shakes his head. "We're not recommending it. Cars are sliding all over the road out there."

I clench my teeth. "Miles. If we have to turn around and go to Boulder, we won't make it back for the wedding."

As the words are out of my mouth, I realize what I'm saying.

I'm going to miss my own wedding.

I start to shake.

Miles looks over at me, drumming his hands on the steering wheel again. He's probably nervous because he's trying to be nice to the police officer, and it's so unlike him to be nice to anyone.

I'm so wired I can't even blink. Behind us, cars are turning around and heading back towards Boulder, their headlights making arcs on my windshield.

He points at me. "Listen. Her wedding's tomorrow morning. At the Midnight Lodge? If she doesn't get there, it's going to be a pretty big deal. She has five hundred guests waiting."

The officer comes closer and shines a flashlight into the car, at me. I give him my most pitiful look.

"No kidding. You two kids are getting married? Mazel tov."

Miles doesn't bother to correct him. "You think it's passable?"

"You'll probably be fine, if you go slow. There's a bunch of yahoos on the mountain going too fast, a lot of stopped cars. Just take your time. I'll let you through."

I clasp my hands together. "Oh, thank you!" I gush. "Thank you so much!"

Miles rolls up his window and waves at him as he motions to another officer, and they guide us through the emergency vehicles, past an SUV that's slid into a mangled guardrail.

And just like that, we're off again.

After a few minutes, I have to say it. Begrudgingly, I mumble, "Thanks."

"For what?"

"For telling the officer we needed to get through and not just giving up."

"Well. It's against my better judgement." His jaw is tight. "And I'm not doing it for you. I'm doing it because I think I'd rather slide off a cliff than have to spend the night with you in Boulder."

I scowl at him. "Same."

He grunts like he's happy with the agreement.

The car feels like it doesn't have any traction. It's slipping over the snow-covered roads, and there are no tire marks here to follow.

"I guess we should go slow," I tell him, rubbing my hands together as he revs the engine to get us up the mountain.

"I get it. I'll go the fastest slow that I can."

I smile. Maybe I don't hate him all that much.

5:46 PM, DECEMBER 6

Well, things were good for a while.

But not long enough.

When Miles said he was going to go fast, I should've realized that term was relative. Miles is careful and calculating. He's slow and decisive. He'll never be a race car driver.

For the hundredth time, I imagine reaching over and stomping my foot on the gas pedal. But he's just as possessive of the pedal as he was of the horn.

I never should've let him have the wheel.

The good? We haven't slid once. And it must be slippery out there, because there are cars all over the shoulders, pressed against the guardrails at unnatural angles.

The bad? We are still at least four hours away from the lodge.

The radio is all static, so we don't have that. Without my car charger, my phone only has about thirty percent charge. Not that it matters, because I can't get a signal up here, anyway.

So the *really* bad? I'm stuck up on this mountain with nothing but Miles to keep me occupied.

Welcome to hell.

"Does your phone have a signal?" I ask him, sighing.

He sucks on his teeth. "I don't know. Let me check," he mutters, his voice leaking sarcasm.

Okay, I should give him a break. It's not the easiest drive in the world, and he definitely shouldn't be peeling his eyes off the road to check the phone in his pocket. The Mini's headlights cut a light about ten feet ahead of us, and the snow steadily keeps falling. There has to be at least eight inches on the ground now, and it's showing no sign of slowing. He looks relaxed, but he always does. He's always had that stoned-out look about him. I've never seen him get excited about anything.

Well, once I did, but I'm not thinking about that night anymore.

We've been driving for a half hour without seeing another soul. I know this route. It's usually busy. I've driven in about a dozen times, especially lately as I've been working out plans for the wedding, but I'm not even sure where we are because it's so dark and visibility is nil.

When I see a sign for the Overlook Pines Rest Stop, I sigh. That's *so far* from our destination, it's not even funny.

Suddenly, our slow pace feels like a snail's pace.

"Can you just step on it a little bit?" I rock in the passenger seat like I'm on a racehorse, as if that'll help us pick up speed.

He rubs at his eye. "I think we should take a break at this rest stop."

I glare at him. "What? No!"

"Yeah. I all but slid the whole way down that last hill. I had no traction at all. You should have chains on your tires. We're not going to get up the next one. I'd rather wait out the storm someplace warm, get some coffee…instead of getting stuck in this car."

I start to hyperventilate. "You're saying…you want to give up? You're telling me I'm going to miss my wedding."

"No. I'm not saying that. This is farther along than if we'd turned back. If we wait in the rest stop, the plows might come through in the morning and we can leave then. You're wedding's not until…when?"

How does he not know this? He received the hand-written, embossed invitation like everyone else, didn't he? "Eleven."

"Yeah. So, plenty of time."

I shake my head vehemently. I have a hair and makeup artist arriving precisely at eight AM to beat my unruly locks and tweeze my wild eyebrows into submission. The spa stuff was just the precursor to the real work that needs to happen before I can walk down the aisle. "No, it's not. You don't get it. I missed the spa day. I have to get myself ready. If I breeze in there at ten forty-five, I'll look like crud!"

He doesn't deny this fact. "But my point is, you'll make the wedding. It sure beats lying dead in a ditch somewhere."

I picture the whole scene. Me, rushing into my wedding with my crazy, frizzed-out locks, my bush-woman brows, like some wild woman. The pictures that we'll show our grandkids, attesting to the fact that Grandpa married a cavewoman.

"No," I mumble, "I want Aaron to look at me and go, 'Wow,' not, 'What the hell is that?'"

"You mean Aaron the Oblivious?"

"What do you mean by that?"

He doesn't answer and doesn't have to. Unless I go in there brandishing a keg or stark naked, Aaron probably won't notice.

Still, with the incongruous image of Aaron's horrified face still marinating in my mind, I shake my head. "No. We need to get there. No stopping."

He lets out a tortured breath, along with something that sounds like *Bridezilla.*

Really? So he's going back to that old standby insult again? I can't take it anymore. "Listen to me, you fucking absolute shithead. I'm not a Bridezilla. This is the single-most important day of my life. Aaron is the most important *person* in my life. I want to look good for him. Do you understand?"

He doesn't answer.

I cross my arms. "Of course you don't. I forgot who I was talking to. Have you ever cared about anyone other than yourself? I mean, you've never even dated anyone."

He narrows his eyes. "I've dated."

"Really? How long was your longest relationship?"

He doesn't answer.

"Yeah. You've hooked up, is what you mean. That's all. Have you ever had a repeat engagement? Hmm?"

I study his face, outlined in the dim glow of the dashboard. He runs his tongue over his top teeth. "Sure I have."

"Right. With who?"

He turns away from me so I can't see his face. I wait for the answer.

He doesn't speak at all.

"Admit it. You can't know what I'm feeling right now because you've never attempted to look good for anyone.

You're lucky you're hot, or else you'd never get any tail at all."

He grins. "You think I'm hot?"

I bite my tongue. My face heats. Did I just say that?

"It doesn't matter, though," I quickly say, hoping to cover up for that slip. "You act like your normal asshole self, and most women can't stand to be near you. You drip your opinions and your ego all over them and make them rue the day they ever met you."

He swings his head toward me, taking his eyes off the road to sweep his gaze over me. I see something different in his eyes. He doesn't say a word, but maybe I've pricked that outer shell, because he looks...incensed.

So incensed, I have to look away.

For the first time, I think I might have gone too far.

There's an arrow for the rest stop to the right. The top half of the sign is draped in snow so it just says STOP EXIT. The lines of the road are hidden under ten inches of snow, and the tire tracks of cars that came before us have been swept away by the wind, so it's hard to tell where the road is.

When he starts to veer off toward the exit, I grip the door handle. I point. "Hey. The road is that way."

He nods. "We're stopping so we can switch. If you want to get back to the lodge tonight that bad, you drive."

"Fine," I say, forcing my chin up. "Bring it on."

He thinks he's so smart. Well, I can drive as well as he can. Probably better. This way, we can stop pussy-footing around and really make up some time.

I've never been to this rest stop, because I've never run into weather like this before. It's not much of a stop. There's a giant, empty lot and a small, square brick building in the corner, lit by a single streetlamp. A sign that says *Restrooms* is all but hidden by the snow.

"Why is there no one here?" I wonder. Surely there are other people waiting out the storm.

"They all had the sense to go back to Boulder."

He draws the car to a stop in the middle of the lot. "Beautiful," I mutter, bracing myself to open the door to make the switch. "Okay. Let's go."

He points to the building. "Mind if I use the facilities?"

I roll my eyes. "If you must."

He puts his skullcap on and throws open the door, letting an icy gust of wind and snow inside. He says something before the door slams, but the wind is too loud.

I decide I'm not going out there in my flip-flops, so I carefully climb over the console, which, in my itty-bitty car, involves the movements of a contortionist. By the time I get there, he's still making his way over to the building, trudging through shin-high snow, his flannel's collar pulled up around his face.

I lay on the horn.

He doesn't turn around, just holds his middle finger up and out to me. I see it, silhouetted so nicely underneath that one bright bulb in front of the building.

What an insufferable ass. I can't believe I actually told him that I think he's hot. I'm surprised he's getting snow on his boots when he should be using his inflated ego to float to the restrooms.

As he disappears into the building, I think about the other thing I said to him, about him being repellant to women once he opens his mouth. I'd never seen him that pissed. Yeah, maybe it was harsh, but it's true. If it bothered him that much, he could change. How hard is it to be kind sometimes? It doesn't even need to be *always*. God knows I'm not perfect either, but still.

He can't possibly know what it's like to care about a person the way I care for Aaron. The first year I was with Aaron, I'd seen different beautiful women leaving Miles' frat-house room, doing the same walk of shame I'd done after my first frat party, every single night. After Miles graduated, when we'd meet up, it was the three of us getting together at a restaurant or bar—Miles never brought along a female friend. Even when we'd invited him to the wedding, we'd added a Plus One to his invitation, but he didn't even add a Plus One to his RSVP.

A lone wolf. That's him. The kind of guy who'll probably be single for the rest of his life.

A complete and total asshole.

No, that's not right, I realize, as I think of the GREs.

It was in March, almost two years ago, prior to the incident that nearly ended Aaron and me for good. Miles had come to town, and since I'd just turned twenty-one, we were all drinking at Gritty's, a local bar I was finally able to go to. I lamented to Aaron that I should probably take the GREs and try to get into the Master's program at CU, because I wasn't sure my degree would get me anywhere. But I didn't know where to start, especially with the math section.

Miles told me that he'd taken them a few years ago when he'd gone back for his MBA, and would tutor me if I needed the help.

I was blown away by the offer. He was so busy with his job, or so I'd thought. I figured he was doing it because he absolutely loved to flaunt that big old brain of his around. So I didn't read too much into it.

I always knew Miles was smart, but that was how I learned he was a genius. He and math went together like peanut butter and jelly. He could work out complex equations in his head, coming up with the answer before I'd even finished reading the problem.

He'd meet me in my dorm, and we'd sit in the common area. He'd driven all the way out from Denver to help me. All we'd ever do was talk math. But Miles was the talk of the all-female floor. Whenever we were together, girls would show up in the common area to gawk at him and try to catch his eye, especially when I told them all he wasn't my boyfriend.

He never bit. He was almost businesslike when it came to those meetings. Once, one of the girls tried to flirt with him as he was leaving, but he shut her down.

Later on, Aaron told me that Miles had gotten perfect scores on all three sections of the GRE. I didn't even know that was possible.

For the record, I *didn't* get a perfect math score, but I did do a lot better than I would've if I hadn't had the help.

Not only that, Miles has always been a prince of a best friend to Aaron. I remember once, at the end of my freshman year, we'd all gone to a party at TKE with the sole purpose of stealing some of their things, which was what the seniors did. While Aaron really got into the game, being the fraternity president, Miles wasn't interested. The plan was for me to distract the TKE guys by playing Asshole with them, while Aaron and some of his other brothers lifted the goods.

I'd played the card game, but unfortunately I'd lost so terribly that I wound up so drunk I could barely stand up straight.

The last thing I remembered that night, as I'd drifted off on the common room couch, was hearing Miles talking to one of the TKE brothers. The brother had said, "And who do we have here?" in a lilting way, like he wanted to get into my pants, and Miles had replied, "My best friend's girl. Touch her, and I'll break your fucking fingers."

Hmm. Maybe I was just a little too harsh to him. He volunteered to help me. He's not *all* bad.

I'm still thinking of the way he'd looked, with his glasses on, nose buried in a book as he tried to help me with an equation, when he appears in the doorway of the rest stop and starts trudging back to me. Of the way he smelled; clean and manly, making something inside me heat up, as much as I don't want it to.

Cool down, girl, you're engaged to his best friend!

By the time Miles gets to the door, my mind is where it shouldn't be—on that night, in his immaculate room, under the snow-white sheets of his futon bed, doing some very dirty things, things no guy with a fear of touching people should have the right to do.

Then he throws open the door, and a shiver grips me. He closes the door and holds out a Milky Way. "Hungry?"

I blink. He scowls, growling, "Sorry. Steak *au poivre* wasn't on the menu."

I shake my head, surprised that he bought me anything at all. I'm starving, but I also have that dress to fit into. And I am going to wear it tomorrow. I'm determined like that.

"Suit yourself." Miles rips the package open.

Trying not to think of Miles eating a delicious chocolate, I throw the car into drive and start to head out, squinting as I try to see the road.

Honestly, I can't.

It's just a sea of white.

There's no telling at all where the road ends and the mountains begin.

That's okay. I can do this.

I'm not going to let the genius next to me, Mr. Perfect GRE Score, be right *again.*

He takes a bite of his Milky Way, and my mouth is watering as I hear him chewing. I haven't eaten any cheat foods like that since Aaron proposed, and I'm not going to start now, when I'm in the home stretch.

"Place was pretty good back there. Warm. Had coffee. Television. Weather said this should be letting up around daybreak."

I sigh. Letting up at daybreak isn't helping us now, when it's midnight-dark, even though it's barely six in the evening. I could do with some coffee. I think about stopping and going in for some, but that's wasting time. If we get on the road now, we can make it back, maybe not for the rehearsal dinner, but so I can have a good night's sleep.

He stretches his seat belt over his broad chest and I hear it click into place. Then he says, "You know, I don't think— Uh, Shorty? That's not the road."

I squint, too tired, worried, and frazzled to think. "What? Of course it is."

He points in a totally different direction than where I'm heading. "*That's* the road."

I start to take my foot off the gas and lean closer to the windshield as I turn the dial to pump up the defrost. "Then where's this lead?"

His lips curve upward and for the merest second, I think he smiled. "I'm not sure we want to find out."

Feeling a knot in my stomach because of his stupid barely there smile, I put the windshield wipers up a notch and press on the gas.

I shake my head as I see the guardrail, up ahead, as well as a level line of white up ahead that has to be the road. I'm heading straight toward it. "We're good."

"Ahhh, no we're—"

He doesn't have a chance to say anything else, because before I know it, there's a massive bump—and suddenly, we're heading downward.

I jam on the break, but the car fishtails, spinning out, sending a flood of snow up onto the windshield.

Miles is shouting orders at me. "Lay off the brake! Steer into it!"

But I just want to stop and I don't know what the hell I'm steering into.

I hear tree branches scraping along the sides, rocks scraping along the bottom of the chassis, and still, the car keeps sliding down into the unknown. In my mind, there's a three-hundred-foot drop at the end of this.

I start to shriek and cover my face with my hands.

6:34 PM, DECEMBER 6

I am so stupid.

I'm sitting in the car, wipers going at top speed, headlights illuminating a snowy pine tree, the branches of which are pressed up against my car's windshield. I'm not sure where we are, because if I look in my rearview mirror, I see nothing but the dull red of my tail lights. I have the heat going on full-blast because I can't stop shivering.

A second later, the door opens. Miles pokes his head in.

"Good news. I don't think your car is damaged. It just went for a little joyride."

He's actually being kind of human to me, which I appreciate, since I feel like shit to the millionth power.

I sniffle. I think I'm getting a cold. Perfect. It's been at least fifteen minutes since the accident and I haven't been able to pry my fingers off the steering wheel. "What do we do now?"

He slips into the car and closes the door, shaking the snow off his hair. A second later, I realize he's holding a piece of Milky Way out to me. I take it and stick it in my mouth.

I have never tasted anything so delicious in my life. Sweet nectar of the gods.

"Better?"

I nod, licking the chocolate from my lips.

"More?"

"Oh, god no! I can't. I have to fit in a dress tomorrow, remember?"

He snorts. "If you ate from now until the wedding, you'd still be fine. Live a little."

I can still smell the chocolate. He's lucky I don't dive into his hands and lick the rest from his fingers. "Don't tempt me. I'm good."

He pops it between his own lips and I watch it longingly until it disappears.

"All right. Here's what we'll do. The rest stop isn't far away. Turn off and lock up your car. We'll wait it out up at the rest stop, and when a plow comes, we'll see if they have a winch and can tow your car out. Okay?"

"Leave the car? But…"

"It'll be fine here. Let's go."

I cut the engine and pocket my keys in my purse. Cold air starts to seep in. Miserably, I look down at my feet. "I'm wearing flip-flops."

He chuckles. "You sure are. Come on. It's not that far."

"Hold on." I reach into the back of the car and take inventory. I may not be the slob Aaron is, but I'm not the clean-freak Miles is, either. I have a little collection of things I threw in the backseat and never pulled out. I find a giant cardigan and wool hat that I'd thrown back there in October, when I'd gone pumpkin picking with Aaron and it'd been too hot. No boots, unfortunately.

I slip them on and nod at Miles, my hand on the door. "I'm ready. Let's do this."

Miles looks up at my hat and shakes his head.

I scowl at him. "You have something against pom-poms?"

"No. If you're *three*."

"When we get up to the rest stop, please go drown your head in a toilet. All right?"

He smirks, and there's that tiny excuse of a smile, like the smile of a guy who's too good to smile at all. But why is it so attractive? Even if it's a smug smile, like he's so proud he's gotten me riled?

Sheez, I need to stop giving Miles that power over me. *Any* power over me. If I'm going to be stuck with him in this rest stop for the next few hours, I need to find my Zen and not let him get to me.

On the count of three, we push open our doors. The wind's not bad down here, because we're on the side of a hill. But the second my bare feet sink down into the icy snow, I yelp.

Oh, god. It's so cold, and it's nearly up to my knees.

I fight to close the door. Squeezing my bag to my chest, I lift my foot high to take a step toward the back of the car, heading up the steep incline.

I take one awkward step. Then another.

Then I freeze. I look behind me, at my footprints, already filling up with snow.

"Oh, no!" I shout as my face is pelted with snowflakes. "Oh, no!"

Miles is already far ahead of me, on the incline. I can't really see where the slope ends and things start to flatten out, but it might as well be a million miles. Because…

Oh, god.

Miles pivots, his hands in his pockets. This is like a Sunday stroll to him. "You realize you've been out in the snow for fifteen seconds?"

"Yes, but...mayday. I lost my flip flop in the snow. Somewhere."

He gives me a look like I'm pathetic. I'm going to cry now.

"And..." I moan miserably. "I can't...my feet. They hurt."

He snorts. "Suck it up, buttercup."

"No, you don't understand. That's why I hate snow. I have Raynaud's." I grimace. Ouch. Ouch. Big, big ouch. The pain is too much. It's like walking on needles. I might as well die. This is a big nope. Can't do.

I twist my upper half around and reach for the door, prepared to dive in, create a little hobbit hole for myself and wait out the storm there. *He* can wait in the nice warm rest stop with the coffee and food and heat and television. Maybe I deserve this.

Before I know it, a hand slips behind my knees and under my armpits, and I'm hoisted up off the ground. I feel a flash of dizziness as my world is upended, and then I'm in the cocoon of his arms. "What are you—"

"I can't listen to you bitch anymore, Shorty." His voice isn't strained in the least. His body is warm as hell, and I lean into the soft, damp flannel, feeling the heat of his body radiating through his shirt.

He climbs the incline with even, measured steps, as if he's been doing this all his life, never once getting out of breath. My feet are pale white, bordering on blue, but my cheeks are burning more when he pulls open the door of the rest stop.

He sets me down, and as I pull awkwardly away from his delicious, masculine smell, I inhale something awful. Acrid and vile, like Pine-Sol mixed with urine. My stomach turns.

"Um. Thanks." As I shake the snow off my clothes, pull off my hat, and start to blink in the bright fluorescent light and bare surroundings, it hits.

The screaming, stabbing, worse-than-death pain in my feet. It's like fire.

"Ow!" Still wearing one flip-flop, I hobble toward a bench in the center of the room and collapse on it.

My feet are bright crimson, redder than the worst sunburn. My toes are purple, almost the same color as my pedicure. But that's nothing compared to the throbbing, burning pain.

Miles walks over to me and inspects them. "Seriously?"

"Look at my feet." I hold them up so he can see them. "It's a *real* medical condition! That's why I hate the snow. I can't go out in it, or...ow!"

Tears of agony spring to my eyes. I pull my feet up and grab them, trying to rub away the pain, but my hands are burning, too. I'd had gloves somewhere in the back of my car. Why didn't I put those on?

"You're a total mess, Cupcake," he mutters, sitting down beside me. "Come on. Give 'em here."

I straighten. He can't mean that. I mean, he's OCD. He doesn't like to touch or be touched. "What?"

He lifts one of my feet, so I have to turn a little, and then he places both of them on his jean clad thighs. He strips off the flip-flop and tosses it on the ground.

He lowers his hands to cover them. His hands are big and so warm.

"What are you—"

"This okay?"

He's…warming up my feet. Okay.

No, more than okay. Aaron's *never* done anything like this. The last time I had a bout of Raynaud's, it was during the honeymoon period of our relationship, when we were each pretending to like the things the other did, so we could show each other how chill and fun we were. We'd gone tubing up at Winter Park and I'd nearly died on the first ride down, when my glove came off. He'd just laughed at me, told me to go sit in front of the fire at the lodge, and went off to do some skiing.

"Oh. Yes. I just didn't know you were okay with touching."

He shrugs. "Seemed like a matter of life or death. Besides, I'll do anything to stop you from bitching." He gives me a little sideways eyebrow-raise.

"Anything? Hmm," I tease.

His mouth quirks in a half-smile.

He slowly presses against my arch, working into the muscle. He isn't just warming my feet. He's massaging them, working in slow, rhythmic motions that make my heart speed up in my chest. Then he works deep into each little toe.

This goes on for the next five minutes. He's extremely thorough and careful. I never thought I had a foot fetish until now. I can't help feeling an odd buzz in my skin, my stomach, and flutters in my chest somewhere in the place where I should have a heart but suddenly have a flapping bird instead.

My feet are fine now. More than fine. They're warm and buzzing, like parts of me that probably shouldn't be. My breath hitches, and my thoughts threaten to return to that night, when he and I—

No. I can't do that.

"That feels good. Are you a professional?" I ask, to lighten the mood.

He blinks, and whatever spell he was under breaks. He lifts my feet up and slides out from under them, dropping them unceremoniously to the floor. "I think they're good now."

"Yes. They're much better. Thanks."

I pull my legs up under me and sit crisscross applesauce on the bench as I look around. There isn't much to look at besides the things Miles mentioned—the lobby is bare except for the bench, a rack of brochures for nearby attractions, a plastic dispenser of free real estate magazines, trash and recycling bins, and a television on a bracket hanging from the ceiling...and oh! A coffee station.

I guess I didn't notice it first because the smell of urine and cleaning solution is so much stronger than the coffee aroma.

I nearly trip over my still-sore feet, trying to get to the little service. The lip of the pot is cracked and there isn't much left, but I grab a Styrofoam cup and fill it. I take a sip. It's awful and wonderful, all at once. I let the bitter taste settle on my tongue and feel the warmth seep into my bones.

Miles has been conducting what looks like a detailed surveillance of the place. He's tried all the doors and is now peering in the windows of a gift shop, the door of which is locked behind a roll-down security shutter. He looks a little on-edge.

"What, you wanted to buy an I Love Colorado magnet?" I ask, making myself as comfortable as possible on the wooden bench.

He points at the television.

That's when I see what's got him upset. The news anchor is talking about a jackknifed tractor trailer, in Dunn's Landing. Which is, incidentally, between us and the Midnight Lodge.

I bring a finger up to my mouth to gnaw on the nail, then yank it away quickly. "Well, they'll probably clear it up overnight."

"Maybe."

Or, maybe not. I know what he's thinking. This has already been the trip from hell. With our luck, they're not going to clear that mess up anytime soon.

And I'll miss the wedding.

No, I refuse to think about that.

Everything's going to be fine.

The hallway leading off the lobby has two doors for the restrooms, one on each side, and two vending machines for soda and candy. The floor is cold concrete, which feels awful against my bare feet. I pad to the closest machine and the first thing I see is popcorn. I lift my purse—and that's when I remember that I rarely carry money. I use my debit card for just about everything.

"You have a dollar?" I call out.

No answer.

I go back into the lobby and look around. Miles is gone.

A second later, he appears from the back door, holding his phone in front of him. "I got a bar out there."

"You did?" I drop everything, reaching for my phone as I rush to the back door. "Where?"

"About ten feet outside the door. To your left."

I go to the door and nearly press my nose against it, trying to make out what's out there. There's a little porch, but other than that, heaps and heaps of snow. I don't want to get my toes frozen again, so I sigh and hold my phone up, moving it in an arc above my head. Maybe I can find some reception inside.

"Did you at least text Aaron?" I call to him as I walk around like a confused Statue of Liberty, trying to find reception.

"Yep."

I wait for him to say more, but I guess I have to pry it out of him. "And?"

"And? He said he'll see you when we get there."

My nose wrinkles. That's it? "What about telling them where we are and that our car's in a ditch? Maybe they can call the state police so they know to come out and help us when the snow stops?"

He nods slowly. Then he says, "No. I didn't do that."

Great. Why am I the only person who seems to think this is a big deal? Maybe if Miles actually had a heart? Or if Aaron had been the one socking all of his money into the day? Or if any of them had seen all the sleepless nights and chewed fingernails I've gone through over this? Maybe then, they'd care?

Ugh. Men. Entirely too blasé about the important things.

I climb on the bench and hold the phone up, almost to the water-stained ceiling. No signal. Of course.

Hopping off the bench, I trudge to the back door. I'll just run out there, quickly send Eva a little bit more detailed text, since it's clear the men in my life have no communication skills.

I push open the door, into a whipping wind that goes right through all the layers of clothes I have on. The concrete floor is coated in a thin layer of wind-blown snow. The building is doing nothing to ward off the rushing wind. Hunching over, I inch to the edge of the concrete porch until I find the bar on my phone and quickly type in: *We're at the Overlook Pines Rest Stop. Car slid into a ditch. Can you call the state police and see if they can send a tow out asap? Spotty reception here.*

A second later: *Oh, honey! Of course. But I hear there is a jackknifed tractor trailer.*

I sigh. *I know. Maybe the tow can come early tomorrow morning. I can still make the wedding then.*

I shiver as another cold wind blows my hair out of the disaster of a bun. Miles is right; I am a wreck, with my crap mani-pedi, my Cro-Magnon eyebrows, my hair all over the place, my one flip-flop.

And it's all my fault.

All because I couldn't settle for chicken wire and wanted to make everything perfect.

No.

It will *still* be perfect. What had Mimi said? It's not so much the event as it is the man. She had a kick-ass time on the boardwalk at Santa Monica, sharing funnel cake with my great-grandfather. I can have a kick-ass time with Aaron, even if I look like a bushwoman. That's what marriage is all about, after all. For better or worse? Plus, even if I get there a little late, I can just have the makeup and hair people do something simple, not the elaborate up-do I had in mind. It'll be fine.

See, Miles? I'm not Bridezilla. I can totally go with the flow.

Another harsh wind blows in. I shudder and type, *Sorry I'm missing the rehearsal. Is everyone bummed?*

A few moments later, she responds with: *It's ok. Everyone's having fun. Aaron brought out the karaoke.*

I smile. Well, that's good. I'd hate them to be sitting around, bored, wondering why they're there. But I shouldn't worry about that. Aaron is the life of the party. Where he goes, everyone's entertained.

My smile fades.

I want to be there. I'm supposed to be there.

With my family. My friends. My fiancé.

This is my pre-wedding extravaganza, something I've been waiting for almost all my life. And I'm not even there to enjoy it.

Sucking back the whirlwind of emotions inside me, I go in. Miles is sprawled out on the bench, legs crossed at the ankle, watching the television as if he's hanging out in his own man-cave. There's some cheesy old television sitcom starting, with a too-cheery jingle. The words *The Facts of Life* show on the screen in big bubble font.

Miles is staring at it, rapt, nursing his own cup of coffee, which is sitting on his chest. The Boy Scout has made a new pot.

My feet are burning again, but I have other things on my mind. I go to the front door and peer out. There's got to be at least a foot of snow out there. I hug my big cardigan over my body and turn back to him. "You think we should do something to let the police know we're here?" I ask. "I mean, the car isn't visible from the road."

"What?" he mumbles, eyes glued to the television. "Smoke signals?"

I shrug. "I don't know. You have any ideas?"

"Yeah. We wait. This is a public rest stop. Someone'll be around eventually."

"But I don't have the time." I reach up and vise my head in my hands. "I feel like this situation calls for some out-of-the-box thinking. There's got to be a way to get there. Work with me, here. You think my dad would pay to have a helicopter airlift us there? Or…I don't know. Maybe we could get a police escort. A police officer could take us there. That one back down the road was kind of sympathetic. What do you think?"

No answer. Not even a blink.

I snap my fingers at him, releasing him from his trance. "So hello? Any words of wisdom, oh brilliant one?"

"Yeah." He nods, then looks out the window, and at first I think he's coming up with this great plan to get us off the mountain as quickly as possible. Then he says, "You take the good. You take the bad. You take them both. And there you have…*The Facts of Life.*"

I stare at him. "Seriously?"

"Yeah. That about sums it up." He gives me that smirk that gets to me.

And that's it. I can't take it anymore.

"I. Hate. You!" I say, lunging at him, ready to shove him until I remember he hates touching.

Oh, fuck it. I don't care. I'll touch him anyway.

I punch him square in the chest, which doesn't even make a dent in his relaxed façade.

That only makes me angrier.

I scream, "I really, really fucking hate you!"

He sits up and crosses his arms casually, watching me stalk back and forth, flipping out. He's eaten at my last nerve and I swear I'm going to kill him.

"You're such an asshole, Miles. You know that? You sit there, all smug, acting like you're better than everyone."

"You want wisdom? Why should I give you any? You'll just go and do your own thing, anyway."

"That's not true! If I—"

"Yeah, it is. I told you we should take Aaron's Jeep. I told you it was going to snow. I told you we needed to stop at the rest stop. And did you listen?"

I press my lips together, fisting my hands on my hips. I want to yell at him harder. For pushing my buttons. For being here instead of Aaron. For making me feel furious in ways I don't even understand. And for speaking the truth because he's right. It's my fault. All of it. And I hate that he knows it too.

He laughs, noticing my disdain. "Okay. Wisdom. How about this? Get real, Princess. There's no knight in shining armor who's going to come and take you down this mountain for your quote-unquote *special day*. You fucked up, despite being warned, and now you're finding out that you're actually not that special, even on your *special day*. So deal with it."

I stare at him, breathing hard.

And then his words sink in, and as usual, they have a way of piercing me right through my center.

Because as usual, he's right.

I don't want to do it. He hates me enough as it is. But I can't help it. My face crumples, my eyes twitch and cloud over, and I know what's coming.

But I can't let him see me cry. I can't let him get to me. He lives to get to people, to worm his way under their skin and make them uncomfortable.

Without a word, I skip into a run and go back outside, where I throw my back against the brick wall and sink down in a heap on the snow-covered ground.

This time, I don't care about the wind or the cold. Let my feet get frostbitten and fall off. Let a gust blow me off the mountain. It's got to be better than being here, with him.

A second later, the door opens a crack. "Hey. Come back in."

I bury my face in my knees, wiping the tears from my eyes with the fabric of my leggings. I harden my voice. "No. I'm good. Just got some calls to make…"

He walks until he's right in front of me, his big hiking boots toe-to-toe with my bare feet. He crouches down and lets out a sigh.

Then he shrugs out of his flannel shirt and lays the big, thick fabric over me, like a blanket, tucking it under my freezing toes.

I can't meet his eyes or he'll know I've been crying.

"Look…I might have spoken out of turn back there…" he starts, scratching at the back of his neck. "I don't know what else to say."

"You've said enough," I mutter, more too my knees than to him. "And you know what? You're absolutely right, Mr. Know-it-All. Mr. Genius. But there's one thing you *don't* know. You can't know what it's like to be me. To be completely ordinary, because you're so special in so many ways. But I'm not. And this wedding? It's my whole life. Call it pathetic, but that's what it is. I don't have an amazing career or an amazing talent like you. I'm just boring old Dahlia Ripley. Yes, I guess I'm hitching all my hopes to this wedding. So call me Bridezilla. I don't care what you think."

He doesn't say anything for a long time.

Then he says, "And then what? What happens after the wedding?"

"Well...then I'll be married to Aaron. I'll be Mrs. Aaron Eberhart."

"So...what? You just give up your own identity?" He looks a little disgusted at that prospect.

"*No*," I mumble. "But together, we'll form a new one. A better one than when each of us is on their own. And maybe we'll have kids, and raise them, and all that. And maybe I'll learn that my talent is in being an amazing wife and mom. I can't wait for that. It means...I mean, Aaron's everything to me."

"You really do love Aaron? For better and worse?"

I meet his gaze, my thoughts flashing to the future I've always thought we can have. "Of course. I'm marrying him, aren't I?"

"Right," he mutters. He straightens up and starts to walk to the door. "Yeah. Come on in. Your feet are going to get cold."

9:06 PM, DECEMBER 6

et me just get this out right now: Truth or Dare is actually not that fun when you're sober.

And when you're trying to forget that you slept with the only other player in the room.

Somehow, though, we've been playing it for an hour. We've been sitting on that same wooden bench, sipping our coffees, pretending to be interested while keeping the game as PG-rated as possible, for obvious reasons.

I've been gradually slumping over on the bench, trying to make myself comfortable, using my cardigan as a pillow and wrapping my lower half in Miles' flannel. I'm trying to ignore that it smells like his aftershave, so masculine and clean I want to bury my face in it. "All right. Truth or dare?"

"Dare."

I roll my eyes. "That's all you keep asking for! I'm running out of ideas."

He shrugs and looks around. "Goddamn. I wish I had a chessboard. Maybe I can make one?"

"God no. So you can beat me again?" I stand up and start to rub my hands together, thinking. "You're doing this dare, and you're gonna like it."

In the interest of keeping the game PG-rated, I haven't asked him to do anything that requires stripping, cursing, lewd gestures, touching me, or thinking/talking about/imitating sex. Thus, basically, we've discovered how to suck the fun clean out of the game. So most of my challenges to him have been athletic stuff, like running around the building three times.

His haven't been much better. He actually had me alphabetize the brochure rack.

I look around, and an idea strikes.

"Okay. Drop and give me twenty push-ups."

He smirks like, *That's all?* Then rolls to the ground and gets on his knees.

"But," I announce, standing in front of him. "every time you go down, you have to kiss my feet and say, *You are not a Bridezilla.*"

He sits back on his haunches and shakes his head. "Fuck. Truth, then."

I clap my hands together. "Really? Okay!"

Actually, that makes the game more interesting. There are a lot of little mysteries in Miles Foster's world. When I was a freshman in college, all of my friends in the dorm whispered about him like he was some kind of celebrity. They all wanted to know what made him tick.

As big an ego as he has, he's surprisingly mum about his background. I'm not even sure Aaron knows much about it.

So here's my chance to get to know him better. I'm grabbing it by the horns. "Okay. You keep making fun of my wedding. If you were going to get married, how would *you* do it?"

He smirks. "That's a big if."

"You never saw yourself married?"

"No, I have not," he says automatically.

I lean forward. "So you don't agree with the institution, or you don't want to tie yourself down to one woman, or…?"

"All of the above."

"Ah. But hypothetically, if you did... ?"

He laughs and scratches his temple as he looks up at the ceiling, thinking. "Hmm. I guess I only want one thing for sure."

"What's that?"

I'm on the edge of my seat, as if this one answer will open him up totally to me.

"Snow. Lots of snow."

I glare at him. "Ha ha. You're a dumbass. Since you're not being truthful, I get another chance."

"I *was* being truthful."

I cross my arms, still glaring at him.

After a brief showdown, he nods once, conceding.

"Okay. Truth. Hmm. Let me think." I stroke my chin as I mentally sift through the possibilities. "Why did you rush D-Phi?"

He raises an eyebrow. "*That's* the burning question you're dying for an answer to?"

I nod.

"Why do you want to know?"

"Because there were the real frat brothers, the guys who really embraced being part of the fraternity. And then there was you. You never went to any of the sorority mixers, you spent more time playing chess with me than you spent in the basement for the parties, and the second you graduated, you left it all behind. So...why?"

He throws up his hands. "I don't know. I didn't get into all that. Not like Aaron. But you know Aaron's been my best friend since fifth grade. He was doing it, so I did it, too."

"Because you didn't want to be left behind?" I make a little pouty face. "Poor baby."

"I don't know." He yawns and blinks, like he's starting to fall asleep. Yes, this game is dull as hell. "Maybe. It was a long time ago."

"Aaron told me you guys met on the recess yard. He said you and he were the only athletic guys in your class so when they chose teams, you were always against each other. So at first, you hated each other. True?"

He nods, a little surprised I know this about him. "True. What else did he tell you about me?"

I wiggle my eyebrows mysteriously. Honestly, not that much, but I like that he's interested. "That your dad moved your family to Boulder from New Jersey when you were ten, as part of the witness protection program or something like that."

His eyebrows shoot up. "Something like that."

"So it's true?"

He shrugs.

"That's kind of badass. Did your dad witness a big crime or something?"

"No. Most of my family was involved in organized crime. My father wanted to get out, so he made a deal with the FBI that he would testify against them in exchange for our protection."

My jaw drops. "Really? Wait…is Miles Foster your real name?"

"What do you mean? Sure, it's my real name. Is it my given name? No, it is not."

My jaw is now on the floor. "What?" I lean closer to him. "That's interesting. So what is it?"

He shakes his head mysteriously.

"Wow. I get it, I get it. But should you be telling me any of that? Isn't that supposed to be secret? Like, if you tell me, you have to kill me?"

He laughs. "Nope. I mean, I guess it is. But who would you tell? It's not a big deal. Besides, the organization got broken up after my father's testimony. Most of the big players are in jail. My grandfather, my uncles…I doubt anyone's looking for me, and if they are, it's not because they want to kill me. I'm blood."

I lean forward. "But they're looking for your dad, right? Since he got them jailed?"

His face falls. "My parents were killed in an auto accident when I was eighteen," he says, shifting back against his seat. "Aaron never told you that?"

I shake my head, stunned. "I'm sorry." I feel like an ass for bringing it up. And no wonder he was driving slow, back there in the snow. "But that means…you're all alone."

He nods.

"You don't care?"

"Not in the least. Because I like myself. There's nothing wrong with liking the company of yourself better than the company of other people. And I'm not completely alone. I have people."

"No girlfriend, though."

"No." He shoots me a curious look. "Why are you so concerned about that?"

"I'm not. Just curious," I say nonchalantly.

"Well, I have other people. I have Aaron."

"Yeah, but you two barely get together anymore."

He nods, staring at the ground pensively. "Like I said. I'm good by myself."

"You don't get lonely?"

"Rarely."

"But in those rare moments?"

He shrugs. "I remind myself how annoying most of the human race tends to be."

"Hmm. Oh, right. And you're not annoying at all."

"That's right."

God, he's such a smug bastard. I want to smack that superior look off his face. I sit instead. "So... Why don't you ever invite Aaron to visit you in Denver?"

He snaps his eyes to mine. "Hey. What's with the third degree? I thought it's my turn."

I guess I did overreach my turn. But once I got started, I couldn't help it. I mean, he's Mafia! Every fascinating thing I find out about him only makes me want to learn more. He's like my exact opposite. My backstory is the historical equivalent of watching paint dry.

I sit back and pull my knees up, digging my toes into the soft flannel folds of his shirt for warmth. "All right. Truth."

He strokes his chin pensively. For my truths, all he's been asking are these really deep questions that require me to think super-hard, which is probably why I have a little headache. "All right. Pretend Aaron didn't exist. If you could date any movie or literary character, who would it be? Who would be your perfect mate?"

"Oh! That's easy. Andy Dufresne."

He lifts his brows, impressed. "*Shawshank Redemption*, huh? Interesting."

"I totally ship that guy. In the movie? When he says that he loved his wife but she used to say he was a hard man to know. That he was quiet and kept things to himself and was this big mystery and ..."

I stop. Because he's listening attentively, nodding along, and I suddenly realize that Andy Dufresne is nothing like Aaron.

And almost *everything* like Miles. Right down to being crafty as fuck with figures and a chessboard.

Blushing, I find a loose thread on my cardigan and start to pull on it. "Anyway... Truth or Dare?"

He straightens and stretches. "All right. You want the truth as to why I never ask Aaron to visit me?"

I pull the hair tie out of my hair and shake out my hair, nodding.

His gaze sweeps over my hair as it tumbles in my face, and for the briefest of moments, I wonder what it would be like to have him reach over and push it out of my eyes. It's been a long time since he's gazed at me like he wanted me; five years, in fact. And yet, up to that moment he first looked at me like this, I'd never experienced anything so thrilling.

Before him, sex was awkward. With him, I learned that it could be pleasurable, intimate, fun. It was like he'd opened up a whole new chapter in my life that night. I wonder if he realizes that.

I'm studying his lips and imagining them on me when out come the words, "I guess you can say I've moved on."

I'm thinking about the way he'd put a finger under my chin and lifted my mouth to his, when his words suddenly register. "What do you mean?"

"I gave him some time, after college. I thought he'd get past it when he finally got out, almost two years ago. But look at me. I'm twenty-five. I've been out of college almost five years. I've spent five years waiting for him to grow the fuck up. It hasn't happened. And rather than letting him drag me down to where he is, I'm happy where I am. Being an adult."

My eyes widen. "But he's getting married. That's adult."

"Yeah. Maybe it'll change him. And if it does, you two are more than welcome to stay at my place downtown. But right now...I don't want to have to ask my maid to clean up vomit in my guest bathroom from a night of hardcore partying. I'm not there anymore."

I blink. I suppose it makes sense, now, why I've been seeing Miles less and less. "Have you told him that?"

He rakes his hands through his hair. "Yeah. Often. He calls me an old fart and tells me I need to loosen up."

"Is that what he said the night of the bachelor party?"

"Yeah. And hell, maybe he's right. Maybe I'm living life the wrong way. But I'm happy with my choice. That's me. I'm not him."

Right. I know that. They might be best friends, but they're nothing alike.

He's eying me curiously. "Obviously it doesn't bother you."

"Well...no, it—"

"You're still young."

He says it like I'm a toddler and he's some ancient, wise elder. "I'm three years younger than you, dude. And yes, it does bother me."

"And yet you don't tell him that. You never told him that. You went along with it."

"I have." Not that it did much good. "Um… What…happened the night of the bachelor party? Why did you guys get back so late? I mean…how much did he loosen up, exactly?"

He presses his lips together and shakes his head, wagging his finger in front of me. "I think you've asked way too many truths, Shorty. It's my turn."

Right. Anyway, even if he isn't on the same wavelength with Aaron, I know Miles wouldn't betray his trust. But then again, Miles is not a liar. He'd tell the truth if I asked him straight out. I just need to wait my turn.

But maybe I don't want to know the answer.

"Okay." I look around. "I'm feeling adventurous. Dare."

"All right." He reaches into his pocket and pulls out a dollar bill. "I need a blindfold."

I raise an eyebrow and lift my hat. "If I put this over my eyes, I can't see."

"All right. Do it."

I slip the hat on and pull it down over my head.

"Stand up."

I stand cautiously, fanning my hands out in front of me. As I do, I feel him flick the pom-pom. "Stop. Where do I…"

I feel his hand on the small of my back suddenly, nudging me ever so slightly ahead. I take a couple of steps. We're heading down the hallway toward the restrooms and the vending machines. I can hear the soft hum of them, in front of me, when he tells me to stop.

"All right. Put your hand out and pick one."

"But—"

"That's the dare. Whatever you choose, I'm going to feed to you."

I frown. "You jerk."

"So make sure it's extra-fattening. You have a dress to fit into tomorrow."

I'd go back like he did and ask for a truth, but I *am* kind of hungry. I wish I remembered where the popcorn was. I put out my hand and it collides with the glass faster than I expected, making my knuckles ache. "Ow."

"Good choice." I hear the sound of the dollar bill being fed into the machine, buttons being pressed, and the buzz as the item is released. It sounds suspiciously heavy, rattling down there in the bottom drawer.

He guides me back to the bench. I sit down, having absolutely no idea what is going in my mouth. I'm kind of picky when it comes to food. Especially since I've been on my diet, I've pretty much sworn off all junk food—

"Open up."

I hear paper ripping as I open my mouth. I'm oddly scared as I feel something hard pass between my lips, and he pops it in.

I chew.

Then I gag. I bring one hand to my mouth and rip off the hat with the other. "Ew. Ew! Good and Plenty? Really?"

"What? You don't like licorice?"

"No!" I rush to the garbage can and spit it out, then rush and take a sip of coffee to kill the taste. "That's vile!"

He pops one into his mouth and chews. "It's not bad."

"You're weird."

"I am *not* weird."

"Sure you are. You know, all the girls my freshman year were always whispering about you, asking all these questions. They thought you were pretty damn looney tunes."

"Did they now?" He doesn't seem offended, just interested. "And what kind of questions did they ask?"

I grin. "Basically, since you were never interested in any of them, whether you were gay."

He freezes with a handful of candy poised between the box and his mouth. Then he pops them in, his brows furrowing a little. "Well, you of all people could've set the record straight on that one."

Now *I* freeze. When I meet his gaze, his deep blue eyes are intent on mine. He's struck me speechless for a moment, and suddenly I know—I *feel* it in every inch of my face—that my cheeks are burning.

I turn away from him. "You remember that?"

He laughs, a grumbling sound low in his throat. "Yeah. Don't you?"

"Well…yes, but…" I'm trying and failing to get control of myself. I must be as red as a tomato.

He smirks. "And it must've been so memorable for you, because the next thing I knew, you were with Aaron."

I don't know why but it feels as if my stomach is in a freefall. I start to babble aimlessly, like I always do when I'm uncomfortable. "Well, I seem to remember that after it happened, you vanished for like, two months. And I didn't realize you remembered. Because we were drunk."

Feeding off that, he doesn't seem uncomfortable at all. "I wasn't drunk. I've never been drunk in my life."

He…really? He's got to be kidding me.

"Were you?"

I glance at him. Of course I was drunk. I wouldn't have slept with him if…

A little voice intercedes at that moment.

Oh, yes, you would have.

The voice is right. The night had worn on and Aaron disappeared without getting me that beer. And the buzz I'd had started to wear off. I couldn't find my friends and I'd left my cell phone in my dorm so he'd brought me upstairs to use his. And, with pretty much all my faculties intact, I'd gone into his bedroom and...fallen completely, irrevocably under his wizard's spell.

I can't think about that right now.

We need to stop going down this path.

"Well...that one time doesn't prove anything. That might have been the time that made you decide once and for all to play for the other team."

He smirks. "Trust me. It didn't."

Only then am I aware my mouth is hanging open, completely dry. "Well, you never had any girlfriends. I know you had women, but no repeat engagements."

"You know that?"

I'm not willing to admit that every time I left Aaron's room while Miles still lived in the frat house, I practically stalked him, seeing all those gorgeous girls leaving his bedroom. I wondered to the point of near madness whether he'd made them come, whether he'd called them "insanely beautiful," whether he'd opened up new worlds of pleasure for them, too.

His eyes are so hot on me that I can't look at him. Even when I look away, I feel them.

When I open my mouth again, my voice is weak.

"Aaron always said you had unrealistic expectations. That you wanted a triple-D model type. And we never talked about it afterwards, so I assumed you were drunk and made a mistake."

He leans forward and puts his forearms on his knees, nodding. "Well, yeah. That's true." I wish I knew what part he's talking about. "I don't know about the triple D, but I have high standards."

I roll my eyes. "Why do you have such an ego? Why do you think no one is good enough for you?"

He thrusts his hands into the pockets of his jeans and strolls casually over to me, so he's looming like a tower—a warm, hot tower of male flesh—right in front of me. "Not true. I have met someone."

I don't know why my heart plummets at the news. "You have? Why didn't you bring her to the wedding, then?"

"Oh, she'll be at the wedding, all right," he says, as I venture a look up at him and his eyes capture mine. They're darker than I've ever seen them. "She's the bride."

A quick flutter sends my heart skipping, and a moment of breathlessness passes through me. His expression doesn't change for the longest time. His jaw is set, his eyes tinged with defiance, like he's just issued a challenge and now he wants me to respond.

My first instinct? I ache to grab his shirt and put his mouth on mine, feel the scratch of his beard and entwine my tongue with his.

But whoa. Where did that come from? And how wrong and awful would that be of me?

I can't say my second instinct, the desire to push him back down on the bench and straddle his hard body, is any better.

It's a good thing we don't have to obey our instincts, because I'd be in so much trouble right now if I did.

Before I can have a third instinct, I notice the color of his eyes has changed. They're dancing now, vibrant blue.

He was joking. Trying to get me to react, which is his specialty.

I shove him. Hard. So hard, he takes a step back.

He chuckles, almost to himself. "You should've seen your face."

"Fucker. I really hate you," I growl, slamming my fists into his hard chest. "Sure, you're so beyond Aaron. You're just as immature as he is!"

He's not laughing anymore. He puts his hands up to block my fists, and when I don't stop, he turns away.

I stomp away, feeling embarrassed and stupid as hell. What was I thinking? It's nearly ten o'clock and I must be exhausted because for a split second, I'd actually entertained kissing mindfucker Miles Foster. Which isn't really even his name. The day before I'm supposed to marry his best friend.

What the fuck is wrong with me? When I pictured my Wedding Day Eve, I imagined a nice night with family, preparing for the adventure of my life.

Not this. This beyond-shitty clusterfuck that makes me want to go outside, tilt my face to the snowy night, and scream like a fucking banshee that I. Am. Done.

Miles Foster can't keep getting under my skin like this. Any more, and I'll never be able to pry him out. Maybe it's already too late.

11:36 PM, DECEMBER 6

Somehow, I manage a little bit of sleep. But it's not the good kind of sleep.

Oh, it's good in that I forget where I am and really do zonk out. It's bad because the second I close my eyes, I dream about that night.

After Aaron left, I expected Miles would talk to me. But a new frat brother took Aaron's place, and Sergeant Shitface started getting into the game again, instructing the new brother which way to throw the ball. My buzz fading, I stood there awkwardly, biting my lip and wondering when Aaron was going to get back.

Around me, the crowd was rapt with beer pong, cheering and laughing. I tried to be interested, but I suddenly looked around for my friends and realized everyone was a stranger. I began to back away, when I looked up.

Miles was now staring at me.

He leaned over, close, but not close enough to touch me. "What did you say your name was?"

"Lia."

He sat up on his stool, elbows on his knees, and hooked a finger at me, like he had a secret to tell me. I waited for him to ask me the same pick-up questions. What's my major?

His voice was gravelly as he said, "Don't stand there. Stand here."

I frowned at him. So he was ordering me around his house like a fucking lap dog. Even so, I moved like he told me to, confused as to why it mattered. "Why?"

He pointed at the game board, just as a Ping-Pong ball flipped into the cup that would've been closest to me, spraying a couple of girls that were standing where I'd been. They shrieked, drenched.

Oh. That answered that question.

I waited for him to say more, but he didn't. And either Aaron had gone overseas to fetch that beer, or he was never coming back. I began to feel like an idiot, sitting there, talking to no one, so I started to meander away.

"Wait," he said, his voice straining over the music. "Don't go."

I frowned. "Why? So you can *not* talk to me some more?"

"Why do we have to talk? It's too fucking loud here. Can't we just be here?"

I blushed. "Um…why?" I asked.

He tilted his head, regarding me like he was seeing me for the first time. "You ask too many questions."

"Because—"

He put a finger to his lips, and I got the feeling that I was like some science project that he wanted to dissect. So I stood there, for maybe twenty minutes more, watching him give the occasional direction to the brother playing beer pong, until the basement got a little less crowded and things started simmering down.

When it did, he leaned in and said, "You're alone."

Duh. "I don't know where my friends went."

"Text them."

I wrinkled my nose. "I don't have my phone."

His eyes drifted over my shoulders, taking in my bare skin, my long hair. I didn't see appreciation in them; just curiosity. "Why am I not surprised that outfit doesn't have pockets?"

I suddenly felt naked. Well, I *was* close to naked, much closer than I was used to, but I'd dressed in order to fit in with my new friends. It was the tail-end of summer, and still hot, so we'd all worn short shorts and tight camisoles to bare our tans. I crossed my arms over my breasts.

He stood up from the stool as he set his beer down. I noticed he hadn't taken a drink from it once. "Come on."

I know, it wasn't safe for me to follow a guy I'd just met anywhere. But for some reason, I never questioned it. I'd come into the basement from the walkout, so I'd never seen the rest of the house. We climbed up a narrow staircase, into a dark-paneled, masculine room that looked like a medieval banquet hall, complete with a massive wooden chandelier, arched doorways, and tapestries.

He walked through it with his head down, unimpressed, but I nearly tripped over a pile of lacrosse gear that had been discarded there, so interested was I in the house. He didn't stop, and as he passed other guys with D-Phi shirts, he didn't say hi to them. I noticed them eyeing him, too, as if he was as big a mystery to them as he was to everyone else.

Then, they gave me a once-over, like, *What do you think you're doing with* him?

As we climbed another wide staircase with ruby-red carpet over mahogany stairs, I glanced briefly at the lines of composite photos of each class of D-Phi brothers, dating all the way back to 1911. By the time I found the most recent one, he whistled.

I didn't get a chance to find him in the picture. I turned to find him all the way down the long hall. "Come on. Keep up."

I peered into some of the open doors as I passed them. Walls decorated with posters of movies and scantily clad women, shelves holding empty alcohol bottles, floors covered in garbage and strewn clothing. The brothers were slobs. The carpet was stained with a rainbow of strange substances and the hallway and smelled like cheese and body odor. It was the exact result anyone would expect of twenty-some guys living together. Music drifted from one of the open doors, and somewhere, there was a rhythmic banging sound. I didn't realize what it was until a girl started to moan.

That knocked me sober.

I was eighteen, and had had sex exactly twice before. Once, just to get rid of my V-card, and the other, because the first time was so awful, I'd decided I must've done something wrong and needed a do-over.

Annnnd the second time had been worse.

So I really had no interest in a third time. Not until I found a guy to totally sweep me off my feet and romance me out of my panties. Someone I knew really well. Someone I maybe even loved.

He opened the door to his room and hung an arm on the knob. I hesitated in the doorway.

"Coming?" he asked, his eyes challenging me.

I took a single step. When I did, he banged on the door and yelled, "Hey, Ross!"

I whirled to see a guy in boxer shorts, stumbling out of one of the rooms down the narrow hall and scratching his balls.

"You bang a girl in a common room again, I'll kick your ass. You left cum stains all over the upholstery. It's yours to clean up. You hear me?"

The guy mumbled something under his breath, shoved open the door to the bathroom and gave him the finger.

He banged the door again with his fist, then rolled his eyes until they landed on me. "If you stand there all night, there's about a ninety-six percent chance a beauty like Ross might try to have his way with you. Your choice."

Good point. I stepped inside.

His room wasn't just a different room. It was like a different world.

The place was immaculate. There was a neatly made futon in the corner. The carpet had recently been vacuumed because I could see the tracks in it. His walls didn't have posters of half-dressed women and obscure bands. The only thing on his desk was his laptop, and a shelf over the desk had a number of trophies for swimming and rugby. There was an entire wall filled with books, the spines neatly arranged...alphabetically?

I was so shocked by it that I forgot my purpose. The next thing I knew, he held his phone out to me. "Your dorm at Williams?"

I nodded and stared at his phone. "I...really don't know anyone's number. I just met all those people."

"Then I guess you're in trouble." His eyes drifted to the phone, where the display showed the time as three in the morning. Where had the time gone? "Campus transportation's done for the night."

I looked around, feeling a little desperate. This was not how my first frat party was supposed to go. Stranded in a fraternity? Great. Would he throw me out on the street, now?

He sat down on his futon, leaning back, then noticed a bit of fuzz on the carpet and plucked it up. Then he fixed me with a curious, lazy stare. I don't think any guy had ever looked at me with such confidence.

"So…Lia. You look a little worried. Something tells me you're not used to trouble. First time away from home, huh?"

Oh, really? Was it that obvious from the way my knees were practically knocking together? He had a window open, and cold air was blowing in, putting goose bumps all over my naked arms and legs. I hugged myself.

"Relax. I'm not going to hurt you. You can stay here tonight and I'll walk you to the bus stop at six, when they start up again."

Stay here? My eyes trailed to the narrow futon. It looked as clean as the rest of the room, but still…

"You can have my bed. I'll sleep somewhere else."

I let out the breath I'd been holding. "Thanks."

He was still watching me, making me so self-conscious I spun, wobbling a little. My eyes snagged on the books on his shelves. They were all classics. As someone considering majoring in English, I was fairly well-read, but he had lots of lesser-known works from the greats. Albert Camus' *The Plague*, *Pale Fire* by Nabokov, and some Jack London I'd never even heard of before. That, and a whole lot of nonfiction.

I wondered if he knew that he came off as super-pretentious. I picked one of the books, flipped through it, then put it back, upside down, to see if he'd notice. "Interesting collection. Are you an English major?"

He shook his head. "Math and Business. Double major."

"I'm thinking of English, myself." Only because I had to. I liked reading. I wasn't sure what I wanted to do with my life.

"Yeah?" His eyes briefly went to the bookshelf. "Second shelf from top. Third from the left. Read that one. You won't be sorry."

I stood on my toes to read the spine. It was *The Alchemist* by Paulo Coelho. "I've never read that one." I stole a look at him, only to find his gaze on me, wandering slowly up my body in a way that made me feel like he'd already stripped me bare. "You're the first person who hasn't tried to talk me out of English as a major."

He shrugged in a superior way. "Read the book."

I eyed him doubtfully. "You're graduating in the spring?"

"That's the plan."

"And?"

"And I'll move to Denver. I already have a job lined up at a place I've been interning at for the past three years. I'll never come back here."

I don't know why that made me sad. He was the first person I'd met at CU who didn't seem to give a shit about drinking and acting older than he was. He had his own drumbeat in his head, and was marching to that. I liked it. I already sensed I didn't feel the need to pretend for him, and if I *did* pretend, he'd call me out on it. "You won't? Why?"

"No reason to."

"Your brothers don't seem to like you very much."

He chuckled and stood up. He reached into his pockets, removing his wallet, his keys, his phone, and setting them down on the table, like he was about to turn in. "No great loss."

"Hmm," I said, trying not to show how impressed I was. I was at that age where I wanted everyone to like me. I felt like I was in high school, talking to my first real adult. I ran my finger along his bookshelf. No dust. "You're very clean."

He walked toward me, stopping so close I thought he'd touch me. Then he went to the bookcase, slid out the book I'd put in wrong, flipping it the right way. "I just like things the way I like them."

"And you clearly don't like people. Why?"

"I like *some* people." He smirked down at me. "But I don't like socializing. I'd much rather sit back and observe."

"Observe what?"

"People. The way they behave. People like you."

I cocked an eyebrow at him. "You weren't even looking at me."

His eyes met mine, and he held my gaze. "Doesn't matter. You don't just observe with your eyes."

So he had been noticing me? Suddenly, I felt like he knew me better than I knew him. Like he understood that I'd spent most of the past few hours trying to figure him out. "And what did you observe about me?"

"You might not want to know. It's not very kind."

I wrinkled my nose. What, did I have a big butt? I knew I wasn't ugly, but I wasn't the most gorgeous woman on Earth, either. "Well, thanks."

"Relax. It has nothing to do with your physical appearance."

I think that was the first of about a million times since that I had the suspicion Miles Foster was some kind of a mind-reader. I looked away and gnawed on my lip. "I've observed things about you."

"Yeah?"

"You like telling your brothers how to play beer pong, but not actually playing it yourself?"

He tilted his head. "I like the physics of beer pong. The game itself does not sufficiently interest me."

Oh, god, he was *definitely* pretentious. It was a wonder to me he'd ever become a brother here, because it was clear his brothers who'd ignored him on the way up didn't think much of him. "And what *does sufficiently* interest you?"

The smirk faded. "You." He reached over and touched my hair, pushing it behind my ear.

"Me? Why?"

His eyes zeroed in on my lips. "You're insanely beautiful, and I get the feeling that's the least interesting thing about you."

If that was a line, it was a damn good one.

He didn't need it. Any woman would easily be his the second he laid eyes on them.

He dipped his finger under my chin and lifted my face to his. Not fast enough for my liking. I went up on my toes and met his mouth with mine.

He seemed surprised by that, but in a good way. Just like I was surprised he didn't taste like stale beer. He tasted delicious, and he felt like all man. His hand slipped under my hair, cradling my skull. I parted my mouth. His tongue flicked inside and entwined with mine. Not gently, either. Hard. All in.

I swear the Earth tilted. I saw and felt things I never had, before or since. So good. He tasted and felt so damn good.

I let out a little groan and we started to kiss more deeply, and soon we were exploring each other's mouths with abandon.

He walked me across the room as we kissed. He retreated, nibbled my lower lip, once, twice. Then he cupped my head between his big hands and went back in, crashing his mouth to mine, thrusting his tongue deep, mimicking sex. This man knew how to kiss. It was the closest thing I'd ever felt to being kissed like a real grown-up, like in the movies, like making love.

The backs of my knees hit the futon, and he wrapped an arm around my back and lowered me onto it, like a prized possession. As he did, he tore his mouth away with a light, sucking sound.

My eyes trailed to the bulge of his erection under the fabric of his pants. I ran my hand over it and let out a shuddery breath. No wonder he had that ego. He was huge.

My pulse quickened.

I dove for his shirt, lifting it out of his waistband. I scrabbled for the buttons on his pants, but he grabbed my wrists and held them, breathing hard. "Whoa. Hold on. You sure about this? How old are you?"

I nodded. "Eighteen."

"Eighteen," he repeated. "And you know what you want?"

"Yes. I want you."

"Yeah?" He gave me the sexiest smile, full of pure male pride. His eyes narrowed. "Jesus. And you're sure?"

Breathing hard, I gave him an exasperated look. He was acting like he'd never hooked up before. "Miles? Shut up and let's go."

He pulled open the button on his pants and motioned me forward with both hands. "All right. Show me where you want me."

I grabbed his waistband and pulled him on top of me.

He fell upon me, caging me under his body and kissing me. I didn't know that he didn't like to be touched, because he surely showed no signs of it that night. He let me run my hands wherever I wanted—down his firm chest, up his broad back.

But he kept his hands in my hair, on my face, in respectful places. I realized he was waiting for an invitation. Because I was only eighteen. It was kind of sweet.

"Miles? Touch me."

"Tell me where."

"Everywhere."

He dropped his hands down my shoulders, and then under my camisole, sliding them up my rib cage, cupping my breasts and tweaking the nipples.

The second he started touching my body, it was like he couldn't get enough. But I was a little self-conscious, especially about my breasts. They were just handfuls compared to other women's.

He lifted the straps over my shoulders, and I stiffened.

He stopped at once and looked into my eyes. "No?"

"I'm just a little…I hate my boobs."

He kissed the top of my breast. "Fuck. How can you hate them? Every little part of you is like candy. Just tell me if you want me to stop."

I didn't. I wanted him to keep going.

He slid my camisole down and buried his face between my breasts. He tongued and sucked on my nipples, and I arched my back. No one had ever done that to me before. I squirmed as he licked and sucked, again and again, biting my nipples until they were hard and sensitive.

He cupped my breasts. "I think they're perfect, Lia. I can spend all fucking night right here."

Then he pushed back, kneeling between my legs on the futon, unsnapping my jean shorts and helping me shimmy out of them.

He tossed them over his shoulder and looked down at me with heavy-lidded, lust-filled eyes. That superior look was gone. Now, he was hungry. "Look at you," he murmured. "Holy fuck, there's not a single part of you to hate. You're beautiful."

He lifted one of my legs and pressed a soft kiss to my inner ankle, then trailed his tongue down the inside of my calf.

I swear I nearly died, right there.

I was wearing just my pink cotton panties and my camisole, but it was down beneath my breasts. I'm sure he could've seen my heart, beating out of my chest. I'd never felt so sexy.

I reached for the buttons of his shirt, and started undoing them, one by one.

He slid open his shirt, I became infinitely wetter. His chest was tanned and lean, a swimmer's body. God, he was so hot.

He growled, "You want this?"

Yes. Yes, oh, yes.

I suddenly blink back to the present and find myself with my eyes dragging open, lying on my back on the hard bench. The man who in my dream had been tweaking my nipples with lust in his eyes is now older, a little bit hairier and grittier, a lot sexier, and…gazing at me with suspicion instead of desire.

I realize he's holding a bottle of water out to me. "Hey. Shorty? Snap out of it. You want this?"

I blink away the last of the dream and sit up. "I…" What are we talking about? Oh. The water. "Don't you want it?"

"Nah. I just saw a plow go by and now I'm thinking that you're right. We should think of putting something outside to signal to rescue workers that we're here."

"There was a plow?"

"Yeah. But it's gone now."

Great. If I hadn't pulled my little stunt driving off the road, maybe we could've gone out and checked to see if the plow cleared the road any. I peer out the doors. The snow seems to only be falling harder, now. There was a line of bushes outside the place when we came in, and now they're completely covered.

"So do you want it or not?" He shakes the water in front of me a little.

I take the bottle. "Thanks. My dad put a safety kit in the back of my car. I think there are flares there."

"Good."

I reach into my bag and hand him the keys. Then I sit up and watch him as he fixes the skullcap over his head. I remember I'm using his flannel as a blanket and ball it up to throw at him. "Here."

He grunts. "Forget it. I'll be back in five."

I watch him head out, flushing because of the way my eyes sort of, of their own volition, drink in the way his ass fills out those jeans. The guy has such a rocking body it's almost unreal. I remember thinking that he must've worked out as I ran my hand down the hard curve of his backside…

Oh, god.

Shivering, I pull my knees and the flannel up to my chin, but that's no good because the flannel smells like him. I throw it down, guzzle some water, and start to pace, still thinking about that night. The way he'd sucked on and worshiped my breasts.

And suddenly it hits me.

Obviously Miles doesn't care about the triple D. He was perfectly *in love* with my breasts. It was *Aaron* who'd asked me once if I ever considered getting implants. Who'd always comment on the tits of girls in the movies we watched. Who'd had posters of top-heavy naked blondes on the walls of his room at the frat. In fact, Aaron didn't even...

What the hell am I doing? Comparing two men, as if I even have a choice?

I made my choice.

I can't do this. Not now. I need to collect myself. I need to get a grip on myself and not allow Miles, nor his ass, nor his words, nor his anything, get to me.

I check my phone. It's nearly midnight. My wedding day. The happiest day of my life.

And here I am, miles away from the wedding site, dreaming about the groom's best friend.

I am so fucking stupid.

Pushing open the back door, I brave the outside to see if I've gotten any more messages, but no. It feels like everyone has just forgotten about me.

Which isn't very different from the rest of my life.

Sighing, I go back inside, just as the front door opens across the lobby and Miles blows in, the safety kit under one arm, holding his hand out in front of him.

He's dripping blood all over the ground, and it's all over the front of his white thermal shirt.

"Oh, god! What happened?"

My eyes trail past him. Outside, the orange flares burn in the darkness amidst the driving snow. So I guess he did that. But how long will they last in that weather?

"Cut my hand on the guardrail as I was trying to get back up," he mumbles. He's motionless, watching it bleed.

"Don't just stand there! Follow me." I lead him to the women's bathroom and turn on the faucet. "Run it under here."

He does as he's told.

I pull the emergency kit from under his arm. It came complete with a first-aid kit. Opening it up, I find gauze, antiseptic, and tape. He turns off the faucet, but the cut, running from the middle of his thumb to his wrist, keeps bleeding. "You might need stitches."

"No, I don't."

"And you're so brilliant, you're a doctor now, too?" I wad up some paper towels and run them under the other sink. "May I?"

He nods.

I point to the counter. "Sit."

He hefts his body onto the counter, between the two sink bowls, and leans back against the mirror. I take his hand, turning it over. I dab at it gently. I try not to let my thoughts wander back to that night as I touch him, even as innocent as this, but it's all I think of.

He winces.

"Does it hurt?"

He shakes his head. "You know how I am."

Right. He doesn't like to be touched.

"It's called tactile hypersensitivity," he adds. "A *real* medical condition."

He says it with the same inflection as I'd told him about my Raynaud's. "But it doesn't mean you shy away from all touch?"

"Not all of it." Not the touching we did, obviously. "I have to expect it. Want it. And then I'm fine with it."

"Oh. I see." He's so close that if I looked up at him, it'd be like a replay of that night, so I stick to my work, bandage and tape the injury as quickly and professionally as I can. "Good as new."

"That was nice of you. But not something you had to do."

I smile. "Well, it's the least I can do, in repayment for your services."

"Services?"

"Yeah. Remember how you always used to take care of me? When I'd be resting in Aaron's room, when there was a party going on? Or that one time, when we'd gone to that other frat, TKE, and I'd drank too much? You always watched over me and made sure no one took advantage."

He raises an eyebrow. "And how did you know about that, if you were asleep?"

"I was resting my eyes."

He shakes his head. "Ah. You got shitfaced too often with Aaron. You did stupid things."

At first, I'm annoyed. Obviously, as sober as he was, he probably catalogued every one of them. "Well, thanks, Dad," I snap.

Then I sigh. I suppose he's right. Just like Miles didn't want Aaron dragging him down, I guess Aaron did drag me into the world of seven-days-a-week partying. My grades weren't anywhere near as good as they had been in high school because I found myself with constant hangovers, which resulted in many missed classes. At the time, I'd thought it made me cool, but now, I see what Miles means. All four years of school kind of bled together into one big party, and I barely remember any of it.

"Okay. Maybe. I knew you disapproved. So I never understood why you did it. You probably had a lot more fun things to do than watching over Aaron's drunk girlfriend. Didn't you?"

He smooths the bandages on his hand and slips off the counter. "Yeah, well. Just looking after my best friend's girl. But any guy who isn't a total asshole would do the same. Don't read into it."

He opens and closes his hand a little, getting the blood flowing again, then catches his reflection in the mirror as I say, "What do you mean? Read into what? Of course I—"

I stop when he suddenly reaches down, grabs the hem of his shirt, and yanks it over his head.

And oh, my lord.

Not that. My heart can't take it.

I'd done my best to avert my eyes at the lodge. But now, I have nothing else but pink women's room walls to look at. And he is like an oasis in the desert. So I can't help it. I get massive eyefuls of him, enough to feed my fantasies for the next decade. He's certainly not the college boy I knew five years ago. He's filled out. He's gone from kind of lanky to completely cut. Now he has a six-pack. And biceps to die for. And…

And I'd thought he was made for pleasure before. Now…

He glances at me in the mirror as he turns on the faucet and throws his shirt under the stream. "This is my favorite shirt."

I catch the flicker of amusement on his face. He can read my expression like a book. Busted. So I tear my eyes away from the wonderland that is his body and stalk, head down, to the lobby, chanting, *Dumb, dumb, you are so dumb,* to myself as my face overheats.

When I'm there, I fan myself and wipe the drool from the corners of my mouth.

Lord, help me. I've got to pull myself together.

A few minutes later, when he appears in the door, he's still shirtless, and I'm no less hot and bothered.

He sits on the bench, his eyebrow cocked in a way that makes me feel like a schoolgirl. "You get any sleep?"

"A little. It's hard," I mumble, looking right at his chest. "Um. The bench, I mean."

Lia, you are such a goober.

He's sitting on the bench in just his jeans, all male ego, manspreading with his arms out along the back of the bench, like he knows he's something special.

I can't look, and I can't *not* look. The war inside my head must be igniting firebombs in my eyes because his mouth is still twisting in amusement.

Oh, he just loves making me pant, doesn't he?

He hooks a finger at me, like he did that first night, when he prevented me from getting splashed by the beer pong game. That's probably why I feel like a fish on a hook, being reeled right in to my doom.

He pats the seat next to him. "You can rest on my shoulder."

My heart feels drawn to that spot, to him, and yet my head's screaming out warnings. I twist my engagement ring. "Put a shirt on."

"Why?" he challenges, eyes drifting down to my ring, which I realize I'm nervously twisting.

I mumble something incoherent about how it'll be more comfortable that way, but he sees right through it.

"Do I scare you? I thought you needed your beauty sleep, Princess."

I sigh. Right. It's just Miles, after all. If I can't trust him, I can't trust anyone.

I sit down on the bench, and he wraps his arm around me. I drop my head on his shoulder. I try to ignore how well I fit in this spot. How even though he's hard, he's also comfy. How good he smells. How every part of my body is tingling. How his fingers are slowly and lightly stroking my upper arm.

I close my eyes and try not to let my thoughts drift back to that night.

Somehow, sleep comes.

2:06 AM, DECEMBER 7

He knelt on the floor and slowly dragged my panties down over my hips. Spreading my legs, he touched my wet folds, gently at first.

I'd been sitting up on my elbows, but the second he started to move his fingers down there, I collapsed down flat. "Oh, god."

"You want this?" he asked, his voice gruff.

My head bobbed.

Rubbing my sex with his thumb, he inserted a finger. I let out a breath. "This?"

I nodded again.

"Hell, you're tight. You're not a virgin?"

I shook my head.

Still pumping me with his finger, he scooped his other hand under my ass and dragged me to the edge of the futon.

I nearly lost it when he dipped his head and replaced his thumb with his tongue. Just one long, lazy lick that tore me to pieces. He buried his tongue deep in me and groaned.

"Miles!" I squealed. "I've never…no one's ever…"

"You want me to stop?"

I shook my head. I most definitely wanted to see where he was going with this.

"Holy shit," he said, kissing my hip bone and settling between my legs again. "If I'm dreaming, don't wake me up. I want to stay here."

And then he planted his mouth on my core and began to suck.

I'm pretty sure that was the closest to heaven I'd ever gotten.

The last thought that goes through my head, as I'm coming out of the dream, is that I've never been there since.

When I wake up, my face is buried in his chest and it feels so good. He's holding me close and his cheek is brushing my hair. His fingers are entwined with mine. He smells so good. I smile and press my lips against his warm skin in a kiss, to taste him, and then it hits me.

Mayday. MAYDAY.

This is Miles. The wrong man.

I pop up like a spring, putting distance between us. His eyes flicker, and he casts a sleepy eye at me before yawning. "You okay?"

So he was sleeping. Good. Maybe he didn't notice I was nearly licking his chest a second ago?

I hope.

"Uh, sure. Just…nightmare."

"Nightmare?"

No, it wasn't one. Luckily, I stopped myself before it became one. "Almost."

He gives me a curious look but doesn't say more. He stands up, stretching as he walks toward the door to peer outside. While his back is to me, I say a silent prayer for the strength to not gawk at his back muscles like a horny sex addict, but wind up succumbing anyway.

He whistles. "A lot of snow out there," he says, rolling his shoulder. "Flares are gone. But I think another plow came through, so that's good."

I tear my eyes away from his body and grab my phone. "I'll see if I got any texts."

I go outside and check. I have one, from Eva: *Just got off the phone with the state police. They know where you are. They're sending a tow first thing in the morning.*

I hurry back inside to tell Miles the news and spot him coming out of the restroom as I appear. His voice is playful. "Guess what?"

"What?" I echo his playful tone.

"You're getting married today."

I'd almost forgotten. Why does that make my heart squeeze, and not in a good way? "Oh. Right."

"Don't worry, Princess. We're going to get you there." He sounds concerned.

He says it like it's just as important to him as it is to me. And at least he's calling me Princess instead of Bridezilla, but I don't know why it still stings. "Right. Eva texted me there'll be a tow truck here first thing in the morning."

I've been waiting for this day for over a year. So why does it suddenly feel like it really is D-Day?

"Cool. See? Nothing to worry about."

I nod and fan my face a little. I need to get a grip. Of *course* Aaron has made me feel good in bed. He's given me plenty of good orgasms. Everything in that department is fine, just *peachy*, so I don't know why the fuck I'm having the distinct feeling like the time with Miles was so much better.

I need to stop my mind from reeling like it is. I wish I had a book to read, to get my mind off him. My mind's going haywire because I'm about to make a massive decision that'll shape the entirety of my life. The grass always seems greener until you take your shoes off and walk through it a while.

Cold feet. That's all it is.

I sit down on the bench and pull my knees to my chest. Talk about cold feet. My toes are so pale they're almost blue.

Suddenly, it hits me. "Miles!"

He's standing in front of the vending machine, rubbing his chin. "Yeah?"

"I just remembered...I don't know why I didn't think of this before. I have a Macy's bag in the back of my trunk with a pair of boots in there. I was going to return the outfit because I wasn't sure they were my style, but they're better than nothing."

He yawns and stretches, then heads to the front door. "On it."

I start to toss him his flannel shirt, but he waves me off again. So the dude's going to go out there half-naked. He's suicidal. I throw it at his face. "Take it. I've had enough of your washboard abs."

He grins at me and throws it on.

"Thanks. Watch that you don't hurt yourself this time." I sit there, massaging the feeling back into my toes, trying not to think about him.

But that's impossible.

He returns a few minutes later. "Uh. Lia?"

I turn my head suddenly, thinking it's got to be someone else.

He called me Lia.

He actually knows my name? My voice cracks. "Ye-es?"

He's looking into the crumpled Macy's bag. "I think you might be better off barefoot."

I hop off the bench and grab the bag from him. "They're not so…" I look inside.

I'd forgotten how awful it was. The vinyl teddy and matching kitten-heeled boots, and the little mask.

"Um…" I blush bright red.

"You're right that it's not your style. Were you actually going to wear this?"

"Well…" I crumple the bag up and flop down on the bench. "Okay. Here's the deal. Aaron told me he had this fantasy. A Catwoman fantasy. And I thought I could…I don't know. I thought I'd make it come true for our wedding night. But then he said something that made me lose my nerve, so I stuffed it back in the car."

He's eyeing me like I'm from another planet. "You're serious."

I nod.

"What did he say to you?"

I shrug. "Well, when I hinted that maybe I'd give it a try for him, he laughed his head off. He said that I shouldn't even try."

He's listening attentively. He doesn't say anything, like he's waiting for the punch line. I feel like I have to go on, so I start to babble.

"It's all right. I'm not sexy. He told me that's fine. I'm the girl-next-door. I'm the girl he wants to spend his life with, right? Not all those other women. So I guess I should be happy with that," I reason cheerfully, opening up the bag.

"Yeah…" His mouth is open like he wants to say more. Then he closes it and his eyes trail to the ground.

"What?" I pull out the boots. They're thigh-high vinyl with little kitten heels, but they'll keep my feet warmer, at least. I slip them on over my leggings as he watches.

"Nothing." He eyes me curiously as I stand up and model them. "So…you're not going to put on the rest of the outfit?"

I stick out my tongue at him. "Ha ha."

"I'm just saying…if you're having trouble deciding. I can be the judge of whether you're sexy or not." He crosses his arms and sucks in his cheek. "Because I can tell you now. That's pretty hot."

"Ew. Stop it." I know he's just teasing me again. But he needs to stop tempting me to think about anything other than the fact that I'm going to marry Aaron in less than nine hours. I'm going crazy enough as it is. "I think I'll pass."

He shrugs and goes back to the vending machine.

"Do you have a dollar I can borrow?" I ask him as I wobble back to the bench. "I'm starving. Those Good and Plenties didn't cut it."

He shakes his head and holds up a single dollar. "My last one."

"Oh."

All right. No problem. I listen to him pressing the buttons for the machine and take a sip of the water he gave me, which is almost gone. I'll fill my stomach with more coffee. The good news is, I'm definitely going to rock my wedding dress.

In less than nine hours.

Ohmigod. I'm getting married in nine hours. I think.

"That's another plow," he suddenly says.

I whip around, stumbling for the doors in those ridiculous boots. Before I can get far, he takes my hand and puts something in it. "Here."

He's outside before it can register in my head…

Twizzlers.

My favorite candy on earth.

I stand there, frozen, trying to wrack my brain. How did he know that? Had I said that during this trip?

No.

Had I said that to him anytime in the past few years?

No, I've barely ever seen him.

He just somehow knew.

Why?

I know, he's telling me I shouldn't read into things. I shouldn't read into the fact that when all his friends were having fun in basement parties, he was spending his time with me, playing chess. That he drove all the way out of Denver to tutor me for the GRE. That he watched over me at the frat. That he knows my favorite candy when I don't even think Aaron does.

But reading into everything is *all* I'm doing.

I'm Bridezilla. Headcase. Shorty. Princess. He hates me.

Doesn't he?

After a minute, I wrap my cardigan around myself and follow him out to the front. I stand under the building's overhang and watch a plow, busily working at the other end of the huge lot. Miles is standing in snow up to his thighs, his hands in his pockets.

The snow is slowing down.

"Does he see us?" I call, standing at the edge of the overhang, where the snow gradually rises to a massive drift that dwarfs the walls of the building.

"Yeah," he says, turning and pushing through the high snow. "But he's kind of being a dick. I asked him if he'd pull your car out but he said he won't. Liability issues."

"Really?" My spirits plummet. "Did you tell him—"

I stop. I was going to say *about me getting married*, but what had he said before? Just because I'm getting married doesn't make me special.

And he's right.

It's not like I cured a disease or ran a marathon or did something that few people can do.

Everyone gets married.

Other than my small circle of friends, no one else gives a shit.

His eyes drop to the ridiculous boots and he gives me a lazy smile. "Well, you might have different results. *Especially* if you put on that full Catwoman getup."

Hmm. He's so funny. He goes back to watching the plow and I stand there, staring at his broad, flannel-clad back for a few moments, trying to pretend that the mere sight of him doesn't make my mouth water.

Then I crouch down and scrape together a little snow, packing it into a snowball. I throw it with everything I have and—contact. I aim for his head but it hits the back of his shoulder.

He whirls on me as I'm scraping together another one. "You want death?"

A person doesn't bring a knife to a gunfight, but that's just what I did. I'm not athletic, and I'm wearing kitten heels in the snow, and Miles is a beast of an athlete who loves the cold.

He cracks his knuckles and gives me a rabid look that tells me I've woken the dragon.

As I throw another one that misses, he reaches into the snow and forms his own massive ball.

I shriek and look for somewhere to hide. I try to hurry to one of the stone pillars under the overhang, but before I get there, a snowball hits me right in the boob.

"Hey! Sergeant Shitface!" I shout as I shake the snow off me. "You may have won the battle but you're not winning the war."

He saunters innocently up to me, his hands in his pockets, grinning. "Think I already secured victory, Private. For someone who doesn't like the snow, you have a lot of it on you."

"You're hilarious." I bend down to reach for more snow. "You want some more of this?"

My answer's a snowball, right on my chin.

I gape. He's fast. "All right. It's on!"

He motions me forward. "Bring it, Shorty."

I reach down, fingers stinging, and mold another snowball. I aim at his head but miss by a yard.

"You call that bringing it?" he taunts.

I frantically grab more snow as one ball hits me on the top of my head, breaking and trickling cold water down my neck. I squeal.

The next time, I trick him, pretending to throw one way, so that he's not expecting it when I unleash the ball into the drift where he's jumped. Snow breaks on his forehead.

I pump my fist. "Yes!"

He lies there, half-buried in a thigh-high drift, frozen in shock.

My triumph only lasts for a second, because in a blink, his expression of shock turns to raw determination. "Now, you are in for it," he shouts, quickly scraping together an enormous snowball, nearly the size of his head.

I shriek and back away, trying to hide behind the pillar, but lose my footing and fall feet-first into a drift, covering my body, head to toe, in snow. I manage to get my own snowball, somehow, and we both hit each other at the same time, squarely in the chest.

By now, I'm too exhilarated to care about the cold.

I can't feel my fingers or toes, but I don't care.

We're not molding the snow into balls now, we're just throwing handfuls of whatever we can grab at each other.

And I'm laughing. Laughing so hard, I can't stop. I feel dizzy and wet and...alive.

I'm lost in a sea of white as he keeps tossing it at me, getting closer and closer as he keeps taunting me about not liking the snow.

"I think you need to cool off," I say to him as he's bending over.

Then I grab the collar of his flannel, which is still kind of open because he hasn't buttoned it all the way, pull it back, and shove a handful of snow underneath, right at the back of his neck.

He points at me with one hand and grabs my wrist with the other. "You're dead."

He says it like he means it. I try to get away but wind up stumbling backward onto the snow, and a second later, he falls on top of my squirming body, throwing more snow onto me, like he means to bury me in it.

I'm laughing so hard I can barely breathe. "Stop. Oh, stop! *Stop*!"

He does. He's not moving. I'm not moving. We're swallowing each other's heavy breaths. His gaze fixes on mine. His nose bumps mine. I feel the warmth of his skin, the soft hairs of is beard on my chin, the twitching of his cock, trapped between us.

I'm going to die.

I'm not cold.

I'm as hot as a human can possibly be without bursting into flames.

I want to be kissed so bad I can taste him.

A cold wind rips though the valley, then, whipping wet tendrils of my hair into my face.

He blinks and rolls off me. "Admit it. I won that one," he says coolly.

I lie there, my heart beating like mad.

What did I almost just do?

Still dizzy, I sit up and look at my fingers. They're blood red. I'm sure my cheeks are probably two cherries. Miles, on the other hand, is completely unaffected by the cold. He's somewhat out of breath, and his lips curl into a smile on his perfectly chiseled face. "Are you giving up so soon?"

"I can't feel my fingers," I admit, trying to bend them.

Looking into my eyes, he takes my hands between his. Despite having handled all that snow, they're perfectly dry. Immediately, my hands warm like my feet had before, aching with a pins-and-needles feeling.

"Better?"

I nod, forgetting how to speak. The only thing I can think about is his hands enveloping mine.

My hands are cold.

But his are the ones that are trembling.

I wonder if he realizes this, because he lets go suddenly and wipes his hands on his jeans, as if he's just touched something gross.

The plowman comes closer and rolls down his window. Miles climbs over the drifts to talk to him, and I follow, tottering along in those ridiculous boots.

I'm soaked to the skin, and it's only when another wind blows that I realize how freaking cold it is. The pain slowly leaks into my fingers and toes.

"Sure we can't get you to pull our car out?" Miles asks.

The guy, an older man with a beard like Santa Claus, except not as white, shakes his head. "Sorry. Been burned before. Not that it matters. There's still a backup on the bottom of the hill that ain't gonna be cleared out anytime soon."

Miles scratches the back of his neck. "Yeah?"

"Yeah. It's a mess."

Miles looks over at me. "She's getting married at eleven tomorrow. At the Midnight Lodge. What do you think?"

The old man regards me carefully, taking in my outfit. "You planning on walking down the aisle in those boots?"

I frown at him. *Just answer the question, dude.*

He laughs. "The way things look down at the bottom of the hill? No way in hell."

I nearly choke on the cold air. "What?"

"Just being honest, sweetheart."

I start to hyperventilate.

Miles climbs closer to the truck, steps on the side-rail, and hoists himself up. "Look. She's freaking out. She might be better off if you agreed to tow her car out of the ditch. Consider it a wedding gift?"

He shakes his head. "Nice try." He throws the plow into drive, so Miles has to hop off. "You two stay warm, now. Congratulations."

The plow lumbers off and Miles gives me an apologetic look.

I start to fan myself. "I can't breathe. Miles. I can't breathe."

"Hey." He takes my flailing wrists and holds them still. "Look at me. This isn't over."

My teeth are chattering wildly. "I'm falling apart. I can almost feel the dark circles popping out on my eyes. I'm going to look like ass on my wedding day. *Especially* if I don't get there on time."

"Look. If you don't get there exactly at eleven, so what? Maybe they can delay it an hour. Or two." He reaches out and pushes a strand of hair behind my ear, showering me in déjà vu. "And there is no way in hell you will ever look like ass. It's not physically possible."

My teeth stop and suddenly I feel warm. "What?"

He drops my hands and clears his throat. "I mean that Aaron would never think you look bad."

But he has. In our five years together, he's never been afraid to call out when he thinks I look awful. I learned that a few months into dating, when I wore purple and he told me it made me look like Barney. It's why I made sure that every time I was with him, I looked my best. I refused to let him near me for a week when I found out I was allergic to shellfish and got the worst case of hives in history. When I had the flu, I also made sure he kept away. When I got that awful haircut right before my senior year of college? I didn't see him for a month.

"You obviously don't know Aaron as well as you think you do," I murmur.

"Maybe I don't," he acknowledges, digging his hands into his pockets. "But I'd say your wedding day would be too late to admit he made a mistake."

I swallow. Exactly. Which is why I'm not thinking of mistakes from here on out. Everything is as it should be.

We walk a few steps toward the rest stop doors.

"Thanks. And thanks for trying. Back there. With the dick. Why do you think it is that everyone thinks we're getting married?"

"No clue."

I give him a sideways glance. "Really?"

He shrugs. "I mean, yeah. Obviously, you're not my type at all."

Oh. So that whole *you're insanely beautiful* thing was just a line. "Right. Obviously you're like Aaron. You may not want the triple D's, but you want the Catwoman. Considering how excited you were by the outfit."

He nods. "Right."

"I'll tell you what. How about I give it to you, and you can get your girlfriend to wear it? That is, if you ever have a girlfriend?"

He shakes his head. "That's nice of you to offer. But again, big if."

"Right. I forgot. One-night stands are more your thing. No one meets your impossibly high standards to warrant that repeat engagement."

He narrows his eyes and growls low, "That again? Why do you care? Because you were one of my legions of hot women? You curious as to how you stacked up against the competition? Is that it?"

I freeze, speechless for a moment. Then I realize I have the perfect out. "You think I'm hot?"

"Ha. Ha." He pulls open the door to the building and lets me go inside. "Maybe you should stop being so curious. You know what they say about curiosity."

Clumps of snow that had been clinging to my clothing drop on the floor as I walk in.

He doesn't wait for me to answer. He scans down to my boots. "It killed the cat...woman."

"Oh. You're such a comedian."

The heat hits me hard, making my skin burn all over. My clothes are so wet, their dampness grating against my already irritated skin. I wrap my arms around my soaked cardigan and shiver.

He watches me. "Come here."

For a second, I wonder if he's going to offer to warm me up again, but he doesn't. Which is a good thing, because I can't accept. Outside, I was mere millimeters away from kissing him again. In fact, I wanted it. A couple of millimeters were all that existed between being a good wife and an awful human being.

I follow him into the ladies' bathroom, my teeth chattering. The second I get in there, he presses the button for the automatic hand dryer and moves me into the stream of it. It's not hugely better, but it helps.

"These boots were a mistake, I think," I say, unzipping the long zipper down my thigh and stepping out of them. They're not snow boots, so they're ruined, and my feet are just as cold as if I were barefoot.

"I could've told you that," he mutters.

I sit on the edge of the counter and lift my feet up to the warm stream of air. Better. "I think you did, Dumbledore."

He chuckles. "Dumbledore?"

Oh, had I said that out loud? Well, it's not as terrible as some names I have for him. "Yeah. Because even when you don't know everything, you know everything. Or at least you think you do."

"I don't know *everything*," he says smugly, leaning against the tiled wall. "Just most things."

I roll my eyes. Shrug off my cardigan, which is heavy with the dampness, and move around, trying to get as much of my body dry as possible.

As I'm doing that, contorting my body in different ways to get close, I glance in the mirror and see him watching me.

His eyes are hot and possessive. As if nothing short of the apocalypse would tear him away.

He's only looked at me like that once before.

The night I met him.

For a minute, I watch him, watching me. His eyes are darkened again, and they're moving over me the same way his hands had moved over me that night, as if tracing the path they'd made, so many years ago.

And that one simple look confirms everything.

He doesn't hate me as much as I thought, either.

3:10 AM, DECEMBER 7

I threw my head back and grabbed ahold of his pillow. I brought it over my face and pushed it down so I could barely breathe. It smelled clean, like the pillowcase had just been washed.

I felt his nose bumping against my folds, his tongue eagerly exploring. No man had been where he was, right now. Instead of being embarrassed, I was burning up, seeing colors behind my eyelids so bright and vivid I felt like I'd died and gone to heaven.

I arched and my hand found the back of his head, my fingers burying themselves in his thick hair.

When he slowly added a finger, pumping it inside me, I went off like never before, panting like crazy. I pulled the pillow off my head and lifted onto my elbows, trying to glimpse this god among men.

He sat back on his haunches, his mouth wet with my juices. "What?"

"I just…" I think I was still coming. "You made me come."

He slipped onto the futon and pulled his jeans and boxers down. "That's the point. Isn't it?"

"Yes, I just…" No one had ever made me come so fast or so hard.

"Come here." He slid his hand in my hair and his mouth met mine. He nudged me back onto the futon and covered me with his body. I felt his cock between us, and I moaned. He felt so good. "You want it?"

I nodded.

He reached into a small table beside the futon and pulled out a condom. He ripped it open with his teeth and rolled it on.

He applied small pressure to my inner thighs, spreading my legs apart, and I felt his knees drop between my legs. He looked up at me, again asking permission with his eyes. Then he blanketed my body with his own, and I felt his every muscle quivering against my skin. He tangled his fingers in my hair and kissed my lips. I felt the pressure of his cock slipping against the wetness of my sex and sucked in a breath, tensing.

He hesitated there.

"I won't hurt you," he whispered, his breath hot on my ear.

"I know." I drew in a breath and held it, waiting for something I couldn't guess. Something world-changing.

And it was. Whatever I'd known about sex before that moment was *nothing*.

He didn't break my gaze as he filled me, slowly opening me up, his every muscle straining and his breath coming hard as he moved. He concentrated, hard, as if every second meant something, and he was committing each of them to memory.

When he was buried to the hilt inside me, I felt one thing I never had with any other guy before.

Treasured.

He leaned into me, kissed the shell of my ear. "This all right for you?"

Until that moment, with him, I never knew sex would be something I could enjoy. I felt a warmth low in my abdomen that I'd never felt before. My sex gripped him, wanting to move with him, wanting more. "Yes. Oh, *yes*."

He let out a groan. "God, you feel good," he said, tangling his hands in my hair.

"Are you feeling better?"

I look up. Miles is watching me from the brochure rack, where he's sucking down his umpteenth cup of coffee and holding a brochure for the Stanley Hotel in Estes Park. Above him, on the TV, some old episode of *Friends* is playing. There hasn't been a news report in an hour.

He gave me his flannel shirt as a blanket again, and I'm actually quite cozy, even though I don't think I'll sleep anymore. My teeth ache from all the pseudo-strawberry deliciousness of the Twizzlers. I tried to share with him, but he insisted I eat them all, "to fatten you up," he'd said. The snow has almost stopped, but no more plows have come through. My phone only has fifteen percent charge, but I'm trying to stop myself from running outside and checking it every two seconds, since it's the middle of the night and probably no one else has texted me.

Situation: Pretty much the same as before.

Wedding: In eight hours and counting, and still looking iffy.

Small Favor: Miles' thermal shirt is dry now, so he's put it back on.

Problem: After that snowball fight, the temperature in the room skyrocketed. And it's just getting hotter, the more I entertain memories of Miles and me. The tension is now so thick I'd need a hacksaw to cut through it.

I resist the urge to fan my face from that last memory and say, "I'm good. And you? How's your hand?" trying to keep my tone conversational and not like I was just remembering us fucking.

He flattens the bandage down on his palm and rakes the hand through his hair. "Can't complain."

We're both getting antsy. I can tell by his rigid posture—his spine is ramrod-straight—and the way he's practically shaking with unspent energy. It's the feeling you get when there's so much to do but your hands are tied behind your back.

I eye him suspiciously. Miles looks like a powder keg, ready to blow. "There's a shocker."

He frowns. "What's that supposed to mean?"

I didn't mean to get into a fight, but my mood's getting worse and worse by the second, the more desperate I feel, and I can't help it. "It's no secret. Mr. Complain-About-Everything."

He snorts. "Yeah? You're one to talk, Bridezilla. You've complained about the snow about four thousand times. Not to mention, my driving. My vending machine choices. Your—"

"Oh, stop it. You won't shut up! Everything I do, you have to have some kind of snide comment on."

"Yeah, well—"

"Stop!" I say, crossing my arms and facing away from him. I wave somewhere behind me. "Just go over there."

"Fine," he bites out, grabbing a bunch of brochures and getting out of my sight.

Yes. This is much better.

He was starting to seem human before, and that was the problem.

I have to hate him.

If we continue hating each other, there's no room for...the other thing.

I watch a little more of *Friends*, but the volume is down so low I can't hear anything but the laugh track. As I'm sitting there, trying not to be hyperaware of Miles behind me, I cross my arms over my chest and feel something hard in the pocket of his shirt.

Reaching in, I pull out the velvet pouch with the rings.

I open it up and peer at them. We'd purchased the rings at the same jewelry store where we'd gotten my engagement ring. We had the opportunity to engrave a small message inside them, so I look at the one I'd written for Aaron: "*No one but you.*" And the date, December 7.

I smile at that. It's true, despite the big fucking my mind's been putting me through. I love him, and Aaron loves me, and it's right. We're going to get married today, and everything's going to be great.

Then I look at the ring Aaron planned to give me.

I squint to see the writing, but there isn't anything there.

It's blank.

I suck in an uneasy breath. Well. I guess I expected that. I'd told him to call the jeweler to tell him what he wanted to have engraved on it, so it could be a surprise to me, and he probably forgot. Like he forgets everything.

It doesn't matter. What does an engraving mean, anyway? Nothing.

But maybe this is just the start. If he can't remember this, what about when the thrill is gone? Will he forget our anniversary? Valentine's Day?

It doesn't matter. Like Miles said, there are five hundred people waiting to see me marry Aaron Eberhart. I've been over all those doubts before. I made my decision.

I open the flap on the shirt pocket and shove the pouch inside. But it won't go in. There's something blocking its way. I find a stiff piece of paper. A photograph, folded in half.

I pull it out and flatten it, a sneaking suspicion on my mind even before I take in the image.

It's a tawdry picture of a long-haired, long-limbed blonde, lying naked on her side, propped up on her elbow, a come-hither look on her face, her giant tits and bald pussy on full display.

Aaron's dream girl.

At first I think, okay, he needed an image to jerk off to, and so he tore this image from a magazine. Aaron always joked that he loved blondes, and I'm too girl-next-door. He always said that was a good thing; I was marriage material, which was way better than being a sex object.

But as I stare at it until it's burned into my memory, until I know it by heart, I notice something hanging in the background.

It's the painting of the Flatirons I bought Aaron last month.

My hand starts to shake.

I haven't been in his bed in two months, because we agreed on that. Because it would make our wedding night special.

So what the fuck was this woman doing there?

I try to run my mind through possible explanations, but I come up absolutely dry.

The most plausible explanation is the one I've been trying desperately to avoid all night.

Aaron has been lying to me. After all this, all those thousands of promises that it would be me and only me...he's been playing me.

My heartbeat thuds in my ears.

I need to ask him to explain himself. Just call him up and get his take. That's what married couples do, after all. They don't jump to conclusions. They communicate.

Even though my irrational side is dangerously close to taking over.

Irrational side wants to punch him in the nuts.

I try to force it down. *Relax, Lia. No need to be freaking out until he's explained.*

But is there any explanation for this? For this, and the condoms, and the lube...

Add that to the fact he'd cheated on me before.

It means one thing.

I'm a big sucker.

Irrational side wins.

I want to scream at him.

I want to kick him in the nuts until he's dead.

But he's miles and miles away.

I turn, slowly, to Miles. He's hunched in the corner of the room, where I sent him, head on his knees. Motionless. He might be asleep.

Miles, the betrayer.

I trusted him. And he lied to me, too.

He didn't come with me to protect me. Or to help me. Or because he wanted to make sure I wouldn't jump to conclusions about the lube.

He came to deceive me. Because Aaron asked him to.

This picture is the reason he's here with me now.

Gathering myself together, I rise to my feet. Taking measured breaths, I walk slowly to where he's sitting, grasping the photograph in front of me.

When I get there, he looks up. "Hey…" he says, cautious.

His eyes drift down to the picture and grow wide.

He might not be Aaron. But he's the next best thing.

"You fucking asshole," I grit out, ramming my foot between his legs, hard, straight into his balls.

3:30 AM, DECEMBER 7

He doubles over, coughing and covering his crotch from further attack. His voice is an octave higher when he breathes out, "Holy shit! What the *fuck* was—"

I hold the picture in front of his eyes. He doesn't look at it. He does everything possible *not* to look.

"Isn't *this* what you came with me for?" I spit out, hardly able to think. My mind is whirling and my head hurts and I think I might throw up.

He straightens, pushes himself up to his feet and doesn't meet my eyes.

"Hello?" I demand, kicking at his feet, though my bare ones do nothing on his boots.

He holds up his hands in surrender. "Okay. Yeah. Aaron sent me to destroy that picture before you found it. Yeah."

I can't even bear to look at it. I try, but it hurts too much. "Who is she?"

He shrugs. "He didn't tell me. Maybe it's an old picture."

"It's not old. I gave him that painting in the background a month ago!"

He looks just as clueless as I feel. "Shit. Really?"

"Didn't he tell you what was on this thing?" I toss it on the ground and cover my face with my hands. "Oh, god!"

"Lia—"

I rip my hands from my face. "So tell me... Has he been cheating on me this whole time?"

"You know I don't know that. I've only seen him twice in the past year."

"And last night? For the bachelor party?"

He presses his lips together. Then he says, "There was a stripper. He might have..." He takes in a breath and lets it out slowly as he looks up at the ceiling. "He was smashed. You know how he gets. They went away for a little while and when he came back, he said that it was his last hurrah and he deserved to enjoy himself."

My stomach does a somersault. Now I really *am* going to be sick. "He slept with a stripper. Two nights before our wedding."

His eyes—hell, his whole face—pities me. He strokes his beard, and I can tell he's searching for the most delicate way to phrase this bad news. "I can't say for sure."

He *won't* say for sure, because it's Aaron, his best friend, and he wants to give him the benefit of the doubt. I've been doing the same. But sometimes you just have to stop putting lipstick on a pig and acknowledge it for what it really is.

Aaron is a pig. My fiancé is a cheating swine.

Oh, god. I can't breathe. I'm alternating between dread and anger, and all that bottled-up energy inside me is about to explode.

"Why didn't you tell me?" I shout at him, shaking. "Why? Do you really hate me that much?"

"Lia, no. I don't. But Aaron—"

"I get it. He's your best friend. But I have news for you." The tears are falling now and I can't see straight. I shove him hard, right in the chest, and he buckles from the unexpected touch. "Your best friend is an asshole!"

"I know. I know he is," he keeps saying, over and over again, so quietly I can barely hear him.

"So why would you... I asked you, if you knew something, would you tell me...and you lied! You said you didn't know anything."

He nods, his face full of pain. "I know. But all I did, I swear I did it for you."

"For me? Are you fucking kidding me?" I can't believe what I'm hearing. It makes me angrier. I shove him again.

He stands his ground and scowls. "Yeah. Listen and stop hitting me for one goddamn second. You want to be married. Right? You're so hyped up on the grand event of getting married that I don't even think you care *who* the groom is, or *what* he is."

I scowl at him. "What? You really don't think I'd care if I was going to be marrying a serial cheater?"

"You don't. Like you said, you love him. He's everything to you. So it doesn't matter, does it? You'll marry Aaron, no matter what. So I thought to myself, the least I could do is give you that day, that event that you want so badly."

I shake my head. "You're insane. I'm calling Aaron right now and calling off the wedding!"

I whirl away from him, stomping toward the bench and sweeping my phone into my hands. I'm glad I have that fifteen percent because that'll be just enough to call off the wedding and tell him to go to hell. I push open the door and find the signal, then punch in the call.

It rings through to voicemail.

Well, of course. It's three in the morning.

Although, if Aaron was the one who was stuck in the snow, and our wedding was mere hours away, I'd make sure to keep my ringer on.

All the more reason I need to do this.

Gnashing my teeth, I hang up. I can't call the wedding off on voicemail.

I wonder if I can call Eva or my mother to wake him up, and that's when the full weight of what I'm doing hits me.

I'm calling off the wedding.

The wedding my father has spent his whole life's savings on. The wedding of my dreams. The wedding where five hundred guests will be wishing me and my husband the best, right before we go off into our blissful forever.

If I call off the wedding, I'll be the laughingstock of everyone I know. Everyone will be talking about the event, and not in a good way. They'll wonder just what juicy thing made me change my mind. Maybe it'll leak out eventually that Aaron was a cheater, and they'll pity me for the rest of my life. No one will ever be able to look at me without thinking of my disastrous almost-wedding.

Not to mention that I'll leave my parents broke and grandchildless for what might be forever.

I gnaw on my lip and realize, once again, Miles is right.

I'd rather not have known.

Even if…oh, god.

Sniffling and wiping the tears from my cheeks, I go inside, head down.

As I slump into my chair, I feel Miles' eyes on me. "What happened?"

I pull my knees up to my chest. "He didn't answer."

"Ah."

He says nothing else.

He's just there: all six feet plus of hot, surly Miles. Occupying space that somehow I want to occupy too; want to get closer to. Making me mad for too many reasons, one of them being that he's giving me that look that tells me he's sort of disappointed in me because I didn't give Aaron a good send-off to hell. I scowl at him. Of course he knew I wouldn't be able to go through with it. Fucking Dumbledore.

But you know what? He may have been right about everything. But I don't have to let him be right about *this*. I have the control here.

I jump off the bench and run back outside, punching in a text. I can call off the wedding via text. If he can stoop so low that he cheats on me right before our wedding, then he doesn't deserve more.

I write: *YOU FUCKING CHEATING, LYING PIECE OF SHIT!! THE WEDDING'S OFF!*

Then I press send.

And that's it.

The second I do it, my finger starts to shake over the button.

Holy shit. Am I really doing this?

I guess I am.

The sky is onyx, and stars are popping out in the sky. No snow at all.

I put my hand on the door to open it, to flaunt the text in front of Miles and tell him I did it, fuck off, he doesn't know me so well, when my phone starts to ring.

It's Aaron.

I'm still trying to process everything that's happened in the past five minutes, but the nuts-kicking feeling hasn't gone away. I jab the display to answer. "Aaron."

"What the fuck, babe? What's going—"

"Don't call me babe. You read my message. I saw the picture Miles took out of your room. Who's the girl in it?"

"What picture?" He sounded sleepy before, but now he's fully awake. "You mean that blonde? I don't know. Really. I don't know."

"Sure, you don't. She just broke in and slept on your bed? Stark naked?"

"No. I mean, you know when I went to Vegas for business last month? A brother of mine used my place, took the picture, and left it for me as a memento. A joke."

I don't hear the rest of the excuse. Sure, it could've happened like that, but he has an explanation for everything. Everything is just so convenient. "Miles told me you sent him to destroy the photo."

"He what?" I can hear him panting on the other end. "Well, fuck. Of course I did. I didn't want you jumping to conclusions if you found that there."

"He also said he thinks you fucked a stripper at your bachelor party."

He's quiet for a moment. "Well, shit. Miles said that? It's not fucking true."

"Then why would he say it?"

He lets out a snort of exasperation. "How the fuck should I know? But I guess I can understand it. I didn't know he'd try to fuck me over so close to the wedding, though. I thought he was over it."

"Over what?" I bite out.

"You," he says. "Don't tell me you didn't know. He's been after you since that first night. He's only bitter because I was the one who asked you out first."

My eyes bulge out of my head. "*What?*"

"Come on, Lia. Don't be stupid. You had to have known," he mutters. "I guess I need to have a talk with him."

I cringe at the thought of the two of them discussing me. Especially since he's deflecting from the real issue at hand.

"No, you don't. This is between the two of us. You always have a perfect explanation for everything. And right now, I'm not sure I can trust you. I don't want to be married to someone I can't trust."

He lets out a breath. "I don't know what else to do, Lia. You know I turned things around after the last time. And I'm sick of you being suspicious of me. It's fucking exhausting."

I want him to fight. I want him to passionately lay out the reasons why I can trust him. I want him to tell me he's going to drive up this mountain and not bring me down until he's proven to me what a stand-up guy he is.

"Just—I don't know. Tell me something that makes me trust you!" I nearly bawl, desperate.

"Like what? There's nothing I can say. You're only hearing what you want to hear," he says, his voice bitter and dull. "You know what? I'm just sick of all this bullshit, it's over. Done. There's no wedding. All right? Fuck you, Lia."

And then he ends the call.

Just like that.

Now, the wedding's truly off.

Instantly, I feel like a piece of shit. The man I've been in love with for five years just told me to fuck off like I was the *enemy.*

But I don't cry. Not right away. Maybe it hasn't sunk in yet.

I don't know how long I sit out here, in the freezing cold, before Miles comes out. He looks at his phone and sighs. I imagine he must've gotten a text from Aaron, because he says, "I don't think I'm the best man anymore."

"It doesn't matter." My voice is hollow. "There's no wedding."

"There's no wedding?" he repeats, dumbly.

"It's off."

He waits for a minute, like he doesn't believe me, like he expects me to tell him it's all a practical joke. Then it seems to dawn on him, and he blinks a couple of times and shakes his head as if to clear it. "You're not kidding. Shit. I'm sorry, Lia."

So many things are combatting in my head that I can't formulate a single thought. I've been planning this event for over a year, and in the space of a few minutes, our engagement just went poof. I don't know how to feel.

"Are you?" I look up at him, hurt, confused, hell I don't even know what I feel...but there's something more. "Why didn't you destroy it?"

Miles drags his hands along his beard restlessly and snaps his eyes to mine. "What?"

"The picture. Aaron wanted you to destroy the evidence. But you didn't."

His lips open for a bit, then he drops his hands at his sides and shrugs. "Maybe I thought she was hot."

That's a lie. I know it as well as I know my own name. Not only can I tell when Miles is lying, I think I can see through every little thing he's been doing since I met him. And it all seems so obvious now that I can't believe I didn't notice before.

"Aaron told me you…" I stop and take a deep breath, my chest squeezing at the thought. "He said you were lying about the stripper because you were jealous of him."

His eyes flick to mine. He lets out a short laugh. "Yeah. Right. Because he's getting married?"

"No. Because he's marrying *me*."

His face turns serious. He's quiet for a long time, and the only sounds are the wind outside, the vague laugh track from the television, and my own heartbeat.

For a long time, Miles says nothing. Then he says, gruffly and quietly, "What do *you* think?"

I swallow, feeling my neck and my whole body heat up in embarrassment and…I don't know what else. "I don't know what to think. It's kind of ridiculous. And yet…" All these images are flashing through my head. Of Miles, sitting with me and playing chess while the party raged downstairs. Watching over me during drunken parties. Giving me Twizzlers when I never told him they were my favorite. "Are you?" I insist.

He doesn't say anything.

"Miles…" I press, gathering up the courage. I take a breath and let it out. "I…" I shake my head, not even believing what I'm going to ask him. What? Whether he likes me? I start stuttering. "Miles. Just call me names," I beg, "say something. Tell me I'm being ridiculous."

I almost laugh at how stupid I sound. Like we're in fourth grade.

He's not looking at me anymore. His eyes are fastened on some spot on the ground. He's gnawing on the inside of his cheek like there's something he doesn't want to say.

"I'm not lying about the stripper," he finally says, throwing up his hands. "I wish I was. I wish he treated you better. I wish he treated you the way you deserve to be treated."

I smile. Well, nice to know one of them has a conscience. "You do?"

He shakes his head slowly, thinking. "Actually…no."

"No?"

"Yeah. No. Actually, I'm glad he treats you like shit."

I ball my hands into fists at my sides, fury rising up within me. And here I was thinking that he *liked* me? "You're *glad?*"

He nods. "Fuck yeah." There's fire in his eyes, just like there's a strange fire inside my tummy from the passion in his gaze. "I wish he hadn't fucked with things the way he did. It was like he wanted to take you from me just to prove he could have you. And then once he did, he dangled you in front of me, treating you like shit, to taunt me. I thought for sure one of these days you'd see that. But all you've done, all these years, is turn a blind eye to the shit he does! I have every right to be pissed the hell off."

I blink, bowled over.

His voice is a low growl. "You know it's true."

"I don't know that. You didn't care. You fucked me, and then you disappeared. It's been five years, Miles. You think you could've said something after that night, if you cared about him 'taking me' from you?"

"You think I knew what the fuck you meant to me then? I had no clue. I was dealing with it, I was dealing with what happened between us, and how the fuck I felt about it—and about you—and next thing I knew, you were out on a date with Aaron."

I stare at him, shocked. "You disappeared for *months*."

"Yeah. That's how I deal with things. But I remember everything. Lia. Every damned thing. About you, that night, and about the way it tore me up the day I saw you with Aaron. But you know what I remember most? That damn night. You. How fucking crazy you drove me. You were too embarrassed, even drunk, to let me take your top off. Even with that little top you had on, you were shy."

"I…" I feel myself flush hot all over. I guess it makes sense. I was so young and innocent. But now, I'm older, and Miles can still make a wreck of me with just a glance. Just a word!

"Don't get me wrong. It was cute. You fucking melted me." He fists his hands at his sides, the fire glowing more blue now in his eyes. "Your taste, the way you moved on me. You were hot as hell. I liked it. I wanted more."

My heart is stuttering in my chest. "You did? But…"

"I know, I disappeared. I was confused. I'd never been knocked down like that before. I didn't know what I was feeling. By the time I realized what I felt was fucking real, you and Aaron were going out and you looked down your nose at me." He smirks at himself, as if angry. "Figured it was for the best. I thought at least one of us would be happy. But now I don't know. It's not getting easier for me. And you love him, but every time he treats you like shit, I feel like I should've done more to tell you how I felt. How I *feel*—present tense."

"Miles, I…"

I can't speak. I can hardly rationalize right now.

Miles. The all-powerful asshole, who thinks nobody is good enough for him. Miles, the guy who pushes all my buttons and more. Miles, the one whose touch I've never been able to forget. Miles, the guy I never have been able to get over—not really.

So who's the hypocrite now? Him for not saying anything? Or me, for pretending it hadn't meant something all this time? For hiding behind a cloak of hate for years when all I really craved was…this?

Him. Now. THIS.

"So that was why I didn't destroy the picture," he mutters, jaw clenching in frustration. "I was hoping, even now, that you'd realize what you have with Aaron will never be as good as what you could've had with me."

I'm frozen again. I still can't speak.

He shoots me a dark look and laughs bitterly. "So you want to know why I don't have a girlfriend? Why it was always the three of us together? Why I've been distancing myself from you two? It's because I realized that night you were it. You were all I wanted. And every minute I spent with you, watching you in Aaron's arms, knowing it was supposed to be me with you…it's only made me more insane, and more and more certain of how fucking totally in love with you I really am."

I shake my head. "You're joking, Miles…and it's not funny. Please don't joke about this again." I clutch my stomach, like that'll stop it from flipping, from burning.

He drags his hands down his face and drops them, shaking his head as he looks at me again. "I wish I was. God, I wish I wasn't in this hell. Did you know I never had a one-night stand before you? And afterwards, my senior year, I slept with fifty, maybe a hundred girls, trying to fill the hole you'd left there.

"I don't have high standards. I only have one standard. She has to be *you*. No one else will ever be enough. I didn't know what I was feeling that first time I saw you. But I know now, and I've known for a long time. Okay, Lia?"

I open my mouth to speak, but nothing comes out.

He's staring at me, holding my gaze, waiting for me to say something, and all I can think is that he has to be joking. This can't be real.

Finally, he points to the door and mumbles, "Well, now that I've said too much and sufficiently humiliated myself, I'm going to go."

He yanks open the door with great force and disappears inside.

4:02 AM, DECEMBER 7

I think we might have slept five minutes, total. I woke up with the sun streaming in through the blinds, his arms wrapped around me, his cock, hard again, nestled against my ass. His fingers entwined with mine, his breathing warm and even on my shoulder.

One, two, three ripped condom packets were scattered over the pristine floor. He'd fed the used ones into an open Budweiser can, the only thing on his night table besides the alarm clock.

It said 7:09 AM. No wonder the rest of the house was quiet. They were probably all still asleep.

I smiled and rolled over, feeling deliciously sore and well-fucked. Like, I finally *got* what all the fuss was about sex.

I peered at his face. Surprisingly, he was even hotter in the light of day, with the trace of a five o'clock shadow on his jaw and his messy hair falling in his eyes.

I kissed his cheek, savoring his yummy smell, and his eyes blinked open. "Hey," he said, his voice gruff. "What time is it?"

"Seven."

He untangled his body from mine and sat up in bed. "Shit. I've got to get to rugby practice."

"Oh." I reached for my camisole. "I'll be out of your hair in a minute."

He stood up, and we did that little fumbling dance around each other, trying to find our clothes. When I straightened to pull on my camisole, I realized he was watching me—or more specifically, my boobs—with this admiring gleam in his eyes. I never liked my chest, but he seemed to love it.

Suddenly, he nudged me back down onto the bed and fell on top of me. "I kind of like you in my hair. In my hair *and* in my bed."

I giggled as he kissed and nuzzled my neck. "I had fun last night."

"Yeah. Me, too."

He glanced at the clock and grinned at me. "I have a little time. Come here."

He delved a hand under my abdomen and swung me around on the bed, lifting me over him so that we were in a sixty-nine. This was something I'd really never done before. I'd never had a guy's cock in my mouth. But as I sucked him off and felt him lapping at my folds, I decided I needed to do this a hell of a lot more often.

I didn't know cocks well, but this up-close-and-personal examination confirmed it: Miles Foster had an amazing cock.

And the way he was working between my legs, lapping at me like I was the most delicious thing ever while begging me to come on his face, it made me orgasm in record time.

I sucked him off, greedily swallowing his salty cum, another college first for me. Afterwards, we lay there immobile, panting, until I climbed over him and kissed him. We were so fucking salty and sweaty and dirty, and I could tell from the satisfied smile on his face that he didn't mind one bit.

A little while later, he kissed my temple and peeled his body off of me.

"Unfortunately, now I really I do have to go. I've got to get down to the fields."

I sat up and looked around for my panties. He found them first, on top of his desk. He handed them to me.

"I can come back," I offered.

As soon as the words were out of my mouth, I felt like a stupid freshman. Was it obvious how desperate I was to be with him again?

But I was sure this wasn't your ordinary one-night stand. This was more like fate. Like he and I had been thrown together for a reason that had nothing to do with the mind-blowing sex we'd just had.

"Yeah. We have parties every night after eleven. Stop by," he said, pulling on his boxer briefs. He sounded so cool again. Too cool and nonchalant, like he did this every night.

"Okay…" I said, scuffing into my flip-flops.

So that was the way these things went. So casual. He didn't have my number or any way to contact me. I wondered if he even remembered my name. So we'd go our separate ways and he might never see me again. And from the way he was acting, it sounded like that was perfectly fine with him.

My whole heart ached with disappointment as I skulked across his museum-like room while he was stripping the sheets from the futon, as if he wanted to erase all memory of me, so soon. "Well, bye."

I reached for the door. I expected him to say something, but he didn't. *I can come back!* Why had I said that? I started to hate myself for saying that. What a loser.

When I got to the bus stop, I remembered that he'd said he would walk me there.

That must've been a line. As was the one about me being so insanely beautiful, and that being the least interesting thing about me. If it *was,* wouldn't he want to see me again and find out? He was so smooth, he must've done things like this all the time.

Yeah, I'd fallen like a stupid freshman. He was ridiculously hot, and the things he'd made me feel in bed? He was a lady killer. He hadn't struck me at first as that type of person, but of course, that's who he was. It wasn't possible for a guy that hot, smart, and good in bed to not have an ego.

So I was a little disappointed when I got back to my dorm. I'd deluded myself last night into thinking that this was a romantic, love-at-first-sight kind of thing. That the reason why I thought he was so amazing was because he was my other half. That he also saw how well we fit together and wouldn't let me get away.

The girls all wanted to know just where I went and who I'd hooked up with. I was embarrassed that he hadn't asked for my number, so I hadn't said a word. They'd all met brothers and had their own adventures, so I listened politely to those, all the while thinking of Miles.

He had me on a string. I had to go back there.

Three days later, when we went back for another party, Miles was nowhere in sight. I realized he wasn't just being cool. He really *didn't* want to see me the way I wanted to see him.

But Aaron was there. And he was really sweet.

He wasn't as drunk as before, and when he offered me a beer this time, he returned with one. We got to talking, and the rest is history.

It's colder than ever outside, but I'm sweating. Miles never told me that I mattered. That he cared.

He'd disappeared after our hook-up. He was always busy, either at the library, or at practice, or class. I don't think I saw him again until two months afterwards, when I'd convinced myself he was a figment of my imagination and had begun dating Aaron.

It's so funny. I can remember everything about that night with Miles but I can't be sure what happened in the following weeks that cemented my relationship with Aaron. I know that in my overwhelming disappointment and heartbreak, I took things super slow with Aaron, insisting we go on dates. I know I fantasized nonstop about being in bed with Miles again. I know that because of Miles, I didn't have another one-night stand, ever again. As good as it was, the aftermath left a bad taste in my mouth. I waited for months before sleeping with Aaron, on the night of the winter formal, which, I seem to remember, Miles never attended.

No, he pulled a complete Casper for the rest of that semester.

And yet he's blaming this on me?

I yank open the door so hard I nearly dislocate my shoulder. I stomp in, ready to give him hell for fucking everything up.

He's standing there, at the other end of the room, hands in his pockets, staring out the window, at the rapidly lightening sky.

He loves me.

Oh, my god.

It's at that moment that the door swings back and slams into my ass and the back of my head because I haven't gone all the way through. It shoves me inside abruptly with a loud thud.

I don't even feel that pain. The pain is somewhere else, somewhere deeper.

Because I think I just might be in love with him, too.

And this is a big, big problem.

"Miles!" I call, my voice cracking, my knees wobbling.

He turns.

I narrow my eyes at him. "Why didn't you ask for my number? Why didn't you want to see me again?" I accuse, clenching my fists. If he was closer, I'd be pummeling his chest. I want to, so bad. "You're too late!" I yell, the words painful in my throat.

"I know. I know I am. I told you. I didn't know what to do. I'd never felt like that before. And when I finally got my head around shit, you and Aaron were together."

I bridge the distance between us, fists still clenched. "Why? Why would you never tell me? Why would you do this to me?"

He looks down at me, his big blue eyes full of pain. "Damn, Lia. I just wanted you to be happy."

I laugh bitterly. "You think this makes me happy?"

His jaw clenches even tighter, a muscle ticking madly in the back. "No. I guess it doesn't."

My stomach knots even tighter. "You're damned right, it doesn't. If you had the chance to do it again, what would you have done? Huh? Tell me! What?"

He stares at me, so intent I suddenly stop breathing, his eyes raking down to my lips as if he's imagining what he'd like to do with them. To own them, like his best friend feels like he does. "I can't do it again, that's the point Lia…and you're in love with Aaron."

"I don't know what I am!" I cry shamefully, furious now. At him, at life, at Aaron, at everything. "All I know is that I wanted more of you. I wanted *you*. I was fucking obsessed with you—but you made me feel like I wasn't good enough."

"I made you feel that?"

"Not that night! The morning after. When you just…bailed. I thought you'd gotten me out of your system and that was that."

His eyes blaze. "You think I'd get you out of my system that fast?"

No. Because the second he asks that, I know that everything *after* was the mistake.

This is what's right.

Miles takes the final step that'll bring us toe-to-toe, and his eyes, continually asking permission, never leave mine. He slips a hand behind my head and pulls the tie from my hair; my hair falls loose over my shoulders.

His hand stays behind my neck. I tilt my face up to his, my breath choppy.

His mouth sweeps over mine, gently.

I've never kissed a man with a beard before. But it feels good. Manly. Hot. Like home.

I practically dive into the next kiss, wrapping my arms around his back and keeping him there. I open my mouth and let him slip his tongue inside.

He licks into me, growling softly. Like this, my mouth, to him, is home too. Then he gets excited, starts devouring a wet path down my throat, delivering hot, hungry nibbling kisses with his beard that would probably tickle if I wasn't so turned on. His tongue trails over my jaw, greedy, starving.

My whole body feels like a bazooka that's just about to go off. Miles tangles his hand in the hair at the base of my skull and draws my mouth back to his. His lips crush over mine and he kisses me, hard, his tongue claiming my mouth. But I'm claiming what I want, too. I throw my whole body into this kiss, because I can feel it everywhere. Crave him like I crave air. And I'm using everything I can to taste, feel, explore, devour him back. Lips. Teeth. Tongue. Hands.

With frustration, with vengeance, with love so intense I can't even call it love yet. Maybe not ever.

Miles groans when he pulls away, maybe surprised I can pack such passion into the way I kiss him.

I ease back, licking my lips, preparing to apologize, when Miles grabs the back of my head and pulls me back to him, his forehead against mine, his breath against mine, his whole voice rumbling against me. "Fucking hell. I never thought you'd kiss me like this again. Look at me like that again."

He backs me over to the bench and then swoops besides me and sits down, dragging me onto his lap like a caveman. I don't even mind, cause I'm already kissing him again with everything I have. The moment he started pulling me to his lap, my mouth had already fastened to his, getting sucked in return. I don't even want to come up for air. I feel like I've missed five years of the way things were supposed to be, like this is my only chance in my life to feel him again.

Nothing else matters; it's like nothing exists but this moment. Me. And Miles. Ever single, ever elusive to me, suddenly very hard under my bottom, very hungry against my lips, craving me back.

God, craving me back so much it's like his whole body is vibrating against me. Strong and pulsing and needing me.

Needing me like I need him. I'm starved of the way he tastes, smells, feels, sounds. I kiss him deeper and deeper, losing myself in him. Determined to have him, determined to get him out of my system.

Who am I kidding? I LOVE him in my system! He's been in there for five years. He's never really left, and now this craving, this need, this feeling, this *connection*, it's stronger than ever.

And I don't think I'll ever be able to really let go.

Miles growls hungrily and breaks the kiss, cups my chin in his big hands. His eyes are on my lips like he's sorry he had to pull away. "What are we doing here?"

He's so adorably clueless.

His hair is falling in his face, his eyes hopeful and fierce on my face, and I reach over and sweep that strand of hair back.

Suddenly I understand something, and I edge a little farther back from him. "Before me…you never had a one-night stand before?"

He shakes his head, presses his forehead to mine. "Before you, they were not sufficiently interesting to me."

"And after?"

He furrows his brows, as if wondering if this is a test. "Like I said, I kept trying to find what I had with you. I kept trying to feel for someone else…the way I felt for you."

I can't breathe.

"Correction," Miles adds emphatically, "*Feel.* For you. Present tense."

His eyes are sexy, hazy, dark. He looks so primal, breathing hard, hard for *me*. I pull my knee over him and straddle him, pressing myself into his erection, my hands on his jaw as I press a kiss to his mouth. "Miles."

He closes his eyes. "God, this is so fucking right," he breathes out, nuzzling my neck, dragging my scent through his nostrils. "Isn't it?"

"Yes. No. I don't know. Right. Wrong. I don't want to think, you won't let me think," I murmur, then I drag my lips over his scruff and tilt my neck to give him access to my throat. "Just kiss me. Please kiss me, Miles."

He reaches a finger up and gently pushes my hair away from my shoulder, gazing up at me like I'm some priceless treasure he can't believe he finally has. His hand slips into the cardigan and grazes my breast through my thin t-shirt. He murmurs, "Here."

I pull the cardigan down, unhook my bra. "Please."

I pull the cardigan off my arms and lift my t-shirt over my head, tossing it aside. I shrug off my bra.

His eyes start twinkling in amusement, as if he can't believe I'm no longer shy, but at the same time is very pleased by this new discovery. Now, I'm straddling him just wearing my leggings, silently watching him, daring him to make the next move.

He fixes his eyes on my breasts and licks his lips, like a boy who's first in line at a sweets shop and can't decide what he wants to sample first.

"Fuck, you've grown," he murmurs, reaching out and brushing his thumb against one nipple. It hardens instantly. His eyes are pure fire on my skin. "How can you not think you're sexy as hell, Dahlia?"

I shiver when he says my full name.

He raises his gaze. His lips tilt in a devastating smile, but then he gets a serious look again. "Is this revenge on Aaron?" he asks, tipping my chin back to force our eyes to lock.

I'm breathless, thoughtless. All I know is *him* right now.

I'm hardly aware of what he just asked me.

When I'm too breathless to answer, Miles growls, slow and rough. "You know, I don't care."

Suddenly he ducks as he squeezes my breasts in his huge, warm hands and buries his face between them. He cups them both and suckles one breast until I go nearly mad, tugging the nipple with his teeth. The wet sounds of his tonguing fill the room as he lavishes attention on my breasts. And I realize I don't care, either.

Sometimes we misjudge situations, think it is more than it is, or don't realize how big it is until it's too late.

Right now, I don't care about anything except the feel of his hands and mouth on my body. His hunger and my own. The urgency in his hands as he tugs my leggings down slightly over my hips. The frantic way I wiggle on his lap, over his erection, until he finds the V of my panties. And how reverently and possessively he cups my sex, rubbing his fingers over me.

I gasp as he delves a finger under the band, flirting along the pubic hair. I had my first Brazilian wax but left a little bit of a landing strip for Hawaii. He touches it and groans in appreciation, pulling an answering groan from me.

He slips between my folds and begins stroking my clit, his eyes never leaving mine.

Forehead to forehead, I rest my arms on his shoulders as he slips a finger into me. I raise myself up to give him better access.

He takes it, pumping the first one, adding another finger. I moan as he moves, faster and faster, rocking back and forth on my knees with his hand moving furiously in my panties.

"Come for me, Lia. You're so fucking sexy when you come."

When I start to, when my insides start to quiver and contract against his hand, he pulls away to watch me, a look of pure male satisfaction on his face.

I come, and I come, and I come, so hard and so long that I swear the mountain around us moves.

I throw myself against him when I finish, hardly able to control my shivering. His hands cup the small of my back and he nuzzles my neck again. We sit there, fused together, my cheek on his shoulder.

5:02 AM, DECEMBER 7

While I sit on Miles' lap, half-clothed, coming down from my orgasm, all these thoughts start to intrude. Playing "Dream Wedding" with my childhood friends, growing up. Memories of all the stupid checklists I'd made to ensure this event was the wedding of the century. All the millions of bridal magazine photos I went through to get everything perfect.

Things on the wedding front are pretty much in the crapper, right now.

But I'm still holding Miles tight, trying to ward out those thoughts and hold on to this last bit of bliss.

"Lia…"

I refuse to let reality leak in. Not now. "No. Don't."

"Then, what? What are we going to do? We have to talk about it."

I shake my head. I don't want to hear this. "No. We don't."

"Really?"

I can't even force my brain to start working right now. I want to just stay in this little bubble of bliss with him. "When the fuck did you become Barbara Walters?" I snarl.

I slide off his knees, grabbing my t-shirt from the ground as I hurry to the bathroom to clean up.

I don't expect him to be right on my heels, but he is.

He grabs my wrist. "Lia. Come on."

"No!" I swat him away. "Just— *Please.*"

He grabs me in his arms, and I struggle so much that I end up pressed with my cheek against the wall. He pushes my hair aside and sinks his teeth into my neck. His kisses trail warm and wet down my neck and shoulder. "Fuck, Lia. I want you. I want you so much I can't think straight."

I drop the shirt.

His hands slip down my sides and lower my leggings and panties to my knees with one swoop. He cups my ass, molding it, kissing it, licking it, slapping it. "*Fuck.* Your ass is perfect. Anyone ever tell you that?" He sounds so aroused his voice is thick and raspy like sandpaper.

I almost laugh. No, no one had told me, not even Aaron. *Finally* all those months of PiYo are being rewarded.

Tugging off my leggings and panties, Miles comes to his full height and nibbles at my earlobe, breathing hard. "I've thought about it. I've definitely admired it from afar. Now I can't take my hands off it. Off you."

I'm shaking with arousal. I've never needed anything or anyone so much in my life. The only thing I can do is nod.

"Yes," I gasp.

I'm really wet and can smell my own arousal. I hear him ripping at and unzippering his jeans.

I shriek in excitement when he pulls me flush to him; his cock pulsing against my ass, slick with my wetness.

He cups my breasts, kisses my shoulder blades, the back of my ear, his hot, deep breaths making my blood boil even more. "Please, Miles…" I push forward against the wall, to let him in.

"You don't need to ask for it, whatever you want is yours."

I feel the tip of his cock at my entrance. "But I don't have anything, Lia," he murmurs, his voice thick with desire.

I meet his gaze over my shoulders. "I'm protected. I trust you," I breathe.

There's a flash of gratefulness in those blue eyes. Like relief. He flips me around to face him, hoists my legs up to wrap around his hips, pushes me back against the wall, and powers in at once, thrusting so hard that I nearly come. I groan.

"God," we say, in unison, as he stays in me. Unmoving for a second. Two. Three.

He slides his nose down mine.

My breath is his breath.

My want is his want.

My heart is his own.

I can't even reason with those thoughts right now. My walls ripple around him even as he pulses inside me. He groans as if he can't take it any longer. Wraps an arm around my ass, clutching my ass cheeks as he pulls out ever so slowly, then slams back in, hip-to-hip.

And we groan again. My groan muffled when he sticks his tongue into my mouth. And we start to have a tongue fucking fest to the same rhythm of his hips, pushing him as fast and hard inside me as he can go.

And it's only then that I admit that I'm in some very deep trouble with Miles Foster, the best man.

But I'll be damned if I can stop now.

6:18 AM, DECEMBER 7

You coming, Lia? You coming for me?
     Miles...!
     Come for me, Lia. Jesus, you're gorgeous, look at me when you come...

I did.

And just the look in his eyes undid me.

God. I've been eaten alive, and I love it.

"Hey," Miles says gently, sliding his thumb under my chin and tilting my face to his. "You okay?"

Suddenly it all hits me. Everything. The fact that it feels so right in his arms, that I never want to leave them. The fact that I'm wet and half naked, smelling of him while he smells of me, my lips raw from his kisses and my heart sore from what I feel.

I shake my head and wrap my arms tighter around him. My tears fall over his favorite shirt, wetting the shoulder and making a small mess. "I don't know."

I don't know anything right now.

All I know is that I don't regret a thing we've just done. And I think that makes me a horrible person.

"Just hold me."

He does. He draws me closer and kisses the shell of my ear, licks away the tears from the corners of my eyes and my cheeks. Nuzzling my neck and groaning, he whispers, "I can't believe you're in my arms."

"Neither can I," I whisper. I love it there, in this little cocoon of warmth with him. It feels so perfect. So meant to be. I thought the wedding would make my life complete, but I can't imagine anything more complete than being here, with him, like this.

I also can't fucking believe what I just did.

My tears become a waterfall.

Holy hell. Did I just fuck the best man on my wedding day?

I am a walking, talking tragedy.

"Even if it isn't going to last." His voice is suddenly so hollow, it shakes me.

He thinks I'm crying for Aaron? I lift myself up and peer into his eyes. "What do you mean?"

He lifts my hand and plants a kiss on my knuckles. "I know you, Lia. You said you love him. You've been with him for five years. You know him better than you know me. Your whole family is waiting for you to marry him. You don't just give that up."

I stare at him, something hard and caustic growing in the pit of my stomach. "And what? You'll just disappear again? That worked out so well for you the first time."

"What can I do? Yeah, you might not be out of my system. I'm too far gone for that. I knew that going in. But maybe I'm out of yours."

I cross my arms, wiping my wet cheeks, hating this whole situation. "You're not."

"All right. But sooner or later, you might be. And how many times have you broken up with Aaron in the past?"

I frown. He's looking at me, expecting an answer, but I'd have to count. It's more than five. College relationships are hard. He was the only one in his frat who had a serious girlfriend. Everyone else was hooking up, getting together, breaking up the next weekend...so we got caught up in that. We weren't exactly stable. "Well, a lot, but what's your point?"

"How many times has he cheated on you?'

"Well..." I swallow. Why is he going into this now? "If you count the time at the bachelor party, two, but—"

"You know that's not true."

I straighten my spine. "I don't know what you mean."

"Aaron told me about it. You kept breaking up with him because you suspected he was cheating on you."

I push on his chest, pushing myself away from him. Aaron told him? So is that what I was? This amusing joke he could tell his brothers about? All this time, he would tell Miles how shittily he treated me, just to hurt him, and *me?*

"And the thing was, every single time, you were right. Every time you were home, visiting your family? He didn't keep his bed empty. But he'd tell you the things you wanted to hear, explain it all away, and you'd take him back. Because you believed what you wanted to believe, not what you knew was true."

I find my leggings and panties on the ground and slip into them, feeling remarkably numb, considering. That chapter of my life is over, even if it isn't over for Aaron. "You're saying he played me for a fool all these years, and you just let it happen. Is that it?"

"I never thought you were a fool. I thought you were in love with him. I thought he didn't deserve you, and I couldn't understand why you didn't think you deserved more."

"You? Is that what I deserved?"

He shrugs.

"I'm used to being treated like shit, Miles. So you probably could treat me that way and I'd put up with it. I mean, I thought you were sometimes unkind to me because I misinterpreted your distance, but the truth is that you always took care of me in ways not even Aaron did. You've been so good to me for the past five years that I wasn't yours. How do I know that you won't treat me the way Aaron treated me, the second I tell you I'm yours?"

"You really think I'd do that?"

"I—I don't know."

"I guess you don't know me well enough, then. Even after five years." He tucks his cock into his pants and shrugs. "That's why I know. You'll go back to him cause it's what you do."

"No," I cry. Because I shouldn't. Because I don't need to fall into that habit again.

"I'm only speaking from what *I* know. I know you want the wedding. And it's there, waiting for you, over the mountain. It's everything you want."

"Not everything." Because I want something more.

"It's the most important thing to you."

I cross my arms over myself. "Don't think you know *me* so well."

He hitches a shoulder, a challenge in his eyes. "Prove me wrong. No one will be happier than me if you do."

"Maybe *I* will be the happiest of all." I meet that challenge in his eyes with a look of defiance.

He stands up and grabs my wrists, pinning them above me against the wall. "We could turn and go back down the mountain toward Boulder. Run away together."

I laugh, but he's not laughing.

"Stop. You know we can't do that."

"Why not?"

"Because you're too anal. And I'm a planner. When I do spontaneous things, I usually end up fucking something up."

"Like now?"

I capture his cool blue eyes with mine. "No. Not now. This is something five years in the making."

"But it's also why you'll marry him. Because you hate it when shit doesn't go to plan."

I wish I could say he's wrong about that. But he's not.

He must see it in my eyes. That little seed of doubt and confusion in me. My mind planning for one thing, my heart screaming for another. My very fear that every time I think I have it figured out, something goes wrong to prove me hopeless.

He groans and kisses my neck again, and as I tilt my head back and let him ravage my throat, wishing we could just run away like he says, when a flash of orange hits my eyes.

A shaft of orange sunlight, streaming through the glass of the double doors.

"Sun!" I say excitedly, pointing.

As he turns to look at it, I realize the reason for me to be excited over that development doesn't exist. Actually, I should be dreading that, now, because it means that the second we get off this mountain, I have to face my family and friends and tell them why we called off the wedding.

And sooner or later, I will have to face Aaron.

Oh, god.

Will he beg me?

Will he convince me to marry him after all?

Do I want him to convince me? Or do I just want him to try so I can finally say, no thank you. You're no good for me, and I think I know what I want, what I truly want, and what truly wants me back at last...?

I try to reach for Miles again, because maybe we don't have to enter the real world. Maybe we can stay here for fifteen minutes, an hour, a lifetime more, the two of us, in this protective little oasis that I'd once believed was a prison.

But he pulls away from me too quickly, tucking his shirt into his jeans and heading for the door. "Yeah. Would you look at..."

He stops when he reaches the door and peers out. His body tenses.

"Holy shit," he murmurs as I comb my fingers through my hair and hook the clasp on the back of my bra. "Guess the road to the lodge must be clear."

"Really?" I ask, slipping on my t-shirt, standing beside him and peering out. "How do you—"

I freeze.

A familiar hunter-green Jeep is pulling into the plowed lot at a breakneck speed, going so fast, it's fishtailing despite the four-wheel-drive.

Aaron's Jeep.

So it appears that I'm going to have to face him sooner than I thought.

7:08 AM, DECEMBER 7

Aaron jumps out of the Jeep, burying his face in his jacket to ward off the whipping wind as he heads straight for us like a bullet fired from a gun.

Shit, meet the fan.

I back away from the door like it's a wall of fire. "Oh, god. Miles…"

He draws in a sharp breath. "It's okay."

But I can't even…Aaron is here.

He came all this way.

So the wedding can't be as done as I thought.

And I'm trying to decide which one of our necks he's going to try to wring first.

I look over at Miles, who's gazing out the window, his eyes narrowed. He jerks back and his eyes find mine, already punishing me for what he knows I'm about to do.

The door flies open, and Aaron appears. His eyes fall on Miles first. "What the actual fuck, Foster? Did you fuck her?"

Miles holds his hands up.

"Answer me! Did you fuck my fiancée on our wedding day?"

He rockets across the room and shoves Miles hard, in the chest. Miles takes a step back and raises his hands in defense.

He's his normal calm self, so admirably together, while I'm shaking like a leaf. "Man. Chill out."

"I'm not going to chill out until we've thrown down, brother," he growls, raising his fists. His voice is low and lethal, unlike I've ever heard. "And I've ripped your fucking head off. She's about to be my wife! What the fuck lies have you been feeding her, you motherfucker?"

"Aaron!" I shout. "Don't!"

Both men glance at me. Miles' posture stiffens, but his eyes soften. "Lia—"

I try to step between them but Aaron grabs me first, pulling me behind him so hard that I stumble back. "Lia. Back off. Let me finish him."

"No!" I try to move but he grabs ahold of my shoulder and keeps me immobile.

"Lia. Stay out of this."

Miles' hands are still up in a defensive posture. His eyes are cold on his best friend. Aaron's probably banking on Miles not coming at him, because I've seen the two of them fight. Miles is bigger and more built. He has always looked like he could topple Aaron with one hand behind his back, like he was letting Aaron win, because Aaron cared about winning more. "We should talk when you've calmed down and have your shit together."

"My shit together?" He scoffs and rubs both of his eyes. "You're fucking my fiancée and you want me to get my shit together?"

Aaron charges, but I grab the back of his shirt before he can and shout, "Don't you harm a hair on each other's heads or I swear to god, I'll finish both of you!"

Miles backs away. He shoots me a dark look and shakes his head almost imperceptibly as Aaron rushes him.

I manage to throw myself between them again, stopping both of them in their tracks. Aaron wraps an arm around my waist and pins me to his side.

"You know what, man. You're not worth it." He sweeps an eye over me as if to check for damage. "Lia, you're coming with me. You and I can discuss this on the ride."

"But I—"

Miles moves forward to stop him from taking me away, but Aaron reaches out a hand, shoving him back.

"Don't. You're not welcome anywhere near the lodge, Foster. Go home."

"Aaron!" I wrench my arm away from him. "Would you just—"

He wags a warning finger in my face. "Not until we're on our way. We'll be late other—"

"But I don't want to marry you!"

He glances at Miles with disgust and puts his hands on both of my shoulders. "I know. I get that. But you're not thinking straight. Listen, Lia. He's been telling you lies, and you owe me the chance to let me explain myself. I promise, Lia. If you just come with me, you'll see."

He smooths my hair, and his brown eyes plead with me.

I have to give him a chance...don't I? I can't let five years go, just like that.

I am so fucking confused right now, I don't know what to do.

All I know is that I've never trusted Aaron, but I've always trusted Miles.

I take a step toward him. "I'm..."

But when I glance at Miles, he's shaking his head. As if disappointed because he knows I mean to go.

And then he speaks. Says, "Go. Lia. Just…go."

He's letting me go. Just like that.

Aaron's pulling me to the door. He yanks it open and guides me outside. I try to glimpse Miles again, but Aaron's in my way.

Outside, the sun is rising and the snow is glistening everywhere. I never thought I'd say it, but it's truly beautiful.

"Where are your shoes?"

I blink in the blinding sunshine and realize he's talking to me. "I, um…wore flip-flops. And I lost one of them in the snow."

He doesn't offer to pick me up, and I don't want him to. I'm confused enough as it is and if he touches me, it'll only make things worse. So I brave the walk to the lot. My feet sink into the snow, but this time, they don't even burn. I'm numb.

Aaron packs me into the Jeep and throws the car into drive. He starts to pull away.

I glance back at the rest stop building, hoping to see Miles. But I don't. Aaron really is going to leave Miles here. "Aaron, you can't…"

"Yeah, I can. I'm too pissed right now. I can't look at him."

"But how's he—"

"Jesus, Lia! He's a grown man. He'll figure it out!" he snaps, jamming his hands on the steering wheel. "Is he really that good?"

I stare at him. "What?"

"You heard me. You think I didn't know? The way you looked at him? The way he looked at you? It went on for five fucking years. I always felt like the odd man out. Always staring at each other like you couldn't wait to jump each other's bones, the second you two were alone."

"I don't…" I stop as it dawns on me. "You thought I was cheating on you with Miles?"

He pounds the steering wheel. "I don't know! I don't fucking know. But you two are the people I'm closest to…so I didn't know. I can maybe stand losing one of you. Not both."

"Wait. You *planned* that whole thing? Sending us together like that? As some sort of test?"

"Of course not. But somehow I always knew this would happen."

He drives on a little while, silent. The roads are snow-covered and slick, but passable. Whatever accident was backing up cars on the bottom of the mountain is gone now. We pass a few cars going the other way.

The four-wheel-drive on his Jeep traverses the snow easily, so it's nowhere near as treacherous as last night. But Aaron's always been a little more reckless of a driver, and he's going fast, so I'm gripping the door handle.

"I fucked everything up, Lia. I know that. I treated you like shit. You are such an amazing woman and I know I haven't always been the man you deserve." He reaches his hand over and touches my cheek. "But I love you. More than anything. I swear, before I was just going through the motions. But when I thought I could lose you this morning, it woke me up. And I want to marry you, in five hours. I want you to be Mrs. Dahlia Eberhart."

"I…I…" I've never felt so confused.

"We have something good, Lia. We've had it for five years. No, it wasn't perfect, but it was good. Otherwise, you wouldn't have said yes when I proposed. And do you really want to disappoint your mom and dad? Your family? My family? I know I don't want to disappoint them, Lia. They love you. They want you to be an Eberhart, too. You belong with us."

"I know…" The Eberharts took me in like family.

Bile rises in my throat.

My stomach clenches as I think of my father. My mother. I'm sure they're going insane right now. And to call the wedding off? How can I do that? Not to mention the wedding party, who socked a lot of money into this weekend, and the guests, who bought me thousands of dollars worth of bridal shower gifts, all of which I'd have to return…

Miles was right, again. The ball's already been set in motion.

Have I really the power to stop it?

Aaron pulls over to the shoulder of the road, reaches down and takes my hand, running his finger over my engagement ring. "Look at me, Lia," he says when I won't meet his eyes.

I do.

"I swear, Lia. I love you so much. It's killing me to think of losing you. That's why I came all this way. After I hung up on you, it hit me. I can't be without you."

I think of Miles, by now, probably wondering how he's going to get back home. I think of how he made love to me on that bench, not an hour ago. How desperate he was, like he'd been waiting to taste me for a lifetime and almost knew that he'd have to die with this one last taste.

I close my eyes and force the memory away.

Aaron opens his arms to me, and I nestle between them. He kisses my cheek.

The embrace feels stiff, like the arms of a stranger.

A day ago, I was so sure I wanted to be his wife. And now…I just don't know.

"Let's make a deal. Whatever happened before doesn't matter. We start here. Fresh. And we won't hurt each other again. Do you like how that sounds?"

I hesitate.

"Lia?" He presses.

I suddenly feel like a dick. I mean, he's trying. He's trying hard, doesn't he deserve a chance? I force myself to nod. "I do."

But I'm not sure if I believe it.

I'm not sure if I can say those words, when the time comes.

We get back on the road. He's driving with the stick shift in his left hand, managing the steering wheel with his knees, so that he can hold my hand in his right. He keeps stroking the back, keeps gazing at me like he loves me.

And I'm not sure.

He wants us to only think forward, but I can't do that. Not with Miles back there.

I feel like I'm already breaking a promise to him.

"Aaron," I say softly.

"Yeah?" he asks, smiling, giving my hand a squeeze.

"Miles has the rings."

He drops my hand, rakes his fingers through his hair, and his posture tenses. "Fuck."

9:28 AM, DECEMBER 7

We've decided to forgo the rings.

After all, my blind insistence on having them is what fucked me to begin with.

It's been two hours since we left the rest stop, and I'm still trying to come to grips with the fact that I left Miles behind.

What we have between us behind.

"I'm just putting this out there right now." I hold onto the strap over the door as Aaron's Jeep careens down the road at breakneck speed. "I'm not going to look that great."

Actually, I'm not just putting it out there right now. I've been muttering something similar since we got on the road.

"You think I care?" he says again, for what must be the twelfth time. "I'm marrying *you*. Not a fucking supermodel."

Right. He keeps saying that. And I keep wondering why I can't stop saying these things. It's not because I'm worried I'll look awful. For once, I don't really care how I'll look for him. I don't really care that our pictures are going to look lopsided without a best man. Put a fucking fish hook on my finger.

I'm done.

I want him to put the brakes on this. On his Jeep, on this whole thing. I feel like I'm falling toward the ground, picking up speed, and there's nothing but concrete under me.

This time, I was the one who bailed.

I was the one who left Miles behind.

The one who refuses to think about what just happened between us because it's so big, I don't think I can handle it.

I'm surprised my heart hasn't burst out of my chest yet. "Aaron." My voice is weak.

He's going seventy in a forty-five, the motor's roaring, and his soft-top is flapping in the wind, so he doesn't hear me.

"Aaron." I say it a little louder.

"Yeah?"

"We're still pretty far away. And you're going really fast. I don't feel safe."

"It's okay. I'm fine. We can make it."

He's right. We can.

But I'm not sure I want to.

"Our family would prefer us to get there alive."

He presses a button on his hands-free on the dashboard. A phone starts to ring, and then a voice says, "Hello?"

It's his dad.

"Dad, it's me."

"Aaron! Where are—"

"Listen to me, Dad. I've got Lia, and we're heading back. But we're cutting it close. I need you to talk to the officiant and the lodge and ask them if it's possible we can delay a little. See what they say."

"Yeah, Aaron, Mrs. Ripley already has. The officiant doesn't have any conflicts but there's another event at the gazebo where the ceremony's being performed, at one. So we have to be out of there by noon."

I check my phone for the time.

"All right. We can make that," he says, just as I'm thinking the same thing.

He hangs up and looks at me. "Never a dull moment, huh? Hope this isn't foreshadowing how our marriage is going to be, huh?"

I try to smile but I feel so frazzled, I can't do anything but stare at the road ahead. The sun is shining bright, the sky is blue as it's ever been, and the snow is melting away quickly. The wet, dark pavement is now visible in spots, and the glare from the sun is giving me a headache.

"I don't know…" I say, gnawing on my lip.

He glances at me. "Oh. Right." He reaches into his pocket and pulls out his phone. "Text Miles and tell him to get your car out of the ditch and haul his ass over here asap."

My eyes widen. "What? No. Not if you're going to—"

"Relax. He's like my brother, Lia. He fucked up, sure. Like I said, I don't care what happened between you two. It's over. But it's going to feel like shit if he's not there."

I can't believe what I'm hearing. "So…you're not going to throw down?"

"No. We are. I was going to save it until after you and I were married but I guess I can't, considering he has the rings, and considering—"

"We slept together."

That shuts him up.

He shifts his position in his seat. "You…what?"

I'm already not so sure I should've said it the first time, so I can't repeat it. "You heard me."

"Yeah, I did." He blinks and shakes his head as if it was a punch in the face. "When?"

"At the rest stop."

He grits his teeth. His voice sounds pained, tight. "All right. Well, one last fling, right? I told you it was over. Jesus, I didn't want to know that. But all right. What's done is done. I only want to think about the future."

Holy shit.

Am I hearing this right?

I suppose he needs to let this fly because he's cheated on me, how many times?

But I don't want him to.

"But Aaron! What if I *can't*?" I bury my face in my hands. "That's a nice thing to say. But just because you say we get to start over doesn't mean we're going to treat each other any better going forward! The underlying problems are still there."

"Underlying problems?" His brow wrinkles, and his voice drips sarcasm. "And what are those? That you like Miles' dick better than mine?"

I shake my head. "No. That's not fair. I'm confused. I just need time to think."

His face turns cold. "You had two fucking years to think, Lia. Now's not the time. Not when everyone we know and love is sitting at the lodge, waiting for us. And I don't care if you slept with the entire male population of CU. I'm making you my wife today."

"But—"

"Lia, are you *trying* to get me to call this wedding off? Is that what you're doing?"

"No, I—" Yes. I guess I am. Because I don't have the guts to do it myself.

Again.

I look over at him. His jaw is set, his face resigned with a grim determination. If my telling him I slept with Miles isn't going to get him to change his mind about today, I guess nothing will.

I'm marrying Aaron.

I open a text to Miles and type in: *Hey. It's me. Lia. Please bring the Mini and the rings?*

I watch the dancing dots indicating he's replying, and then: *I'm pretty sure you left something else here with me. But if you don't mind, I'm keeping that.*

What the hell is that supposed to mean?

I feel my body. Did I leave my panties there? No. I'm wearing my panties. I'm wearing my bra. All my clothes. What the hell did I forget? He sounds like he needs it, whatever it is, so I guess he can have it. I suppose he always knew Aaron would never get married without him. No matter what he did.

I wipe some hair from my face and realize I'm sweating.

When I imagined my wedding, I imagined romance, love, beauty. A fairy tale.

But this wedding is going to be the biggest three-ring circus there ever was. And I'm going to be the clown in the center ring.

10:38 AM, DECEMBER 7

Aaron and I don't talk much after that. He has the fan on, because we're both sweating and tense. When the Midnight Lodge comes into view on the horizon, he pumps his fist. "Haha! Told you I'd get us there."

I open up a text to Eva and type in: *Almost there. ETA: 5 minutes*

She responds with: *We have everything ready for you. Plus a double mimosa because I think you'll need it.*

I smile nervously. She has no idea. I've never needed a drink so much. But I think I might do better with a double shot of straight vodka. *Thanks.*

Aaron coasts into the lot and pulls in under the overhang by reception. I open the door and jump out before he fully comes to a stop, nearly careening into a line of luggage carts. Eva, my mother, Natalie, and Cara are waiting for me. The bridesmaids are all in their aqua-blue dresses, and mother is wearing the sequined dress she had special ordered for the occasion, and they all look so breathtakingly lovely that I want to cry.

This day, the day I saw them all assembled and dressed to the nines, was supposed to be so different. I wasn't supposed to be such a mess. Inside and out.

Eva hugs me tight. "Oh, honey! Don't worry. It's under control. Come on."

It's a mad dash to the bridal suite, where everything's been set up for me and my bridesmaids to get ready. When I'm rushing down the hall, it occurs to me that I never said anything to Aaron as he dropped me off, and the next time I see him, I'll be walking down the aisle.

I trip over my bare feet, but Eva holds me up. My mother says that my father's assembling everyone outside by the gazebo underneath the mountains, and that if we can get down there before eleven-thirty, everything will be fine.

My best friend rips open the double doors to the bridal suite and hands me a mimosa. I chug it. Like Eva promised, it's extra-strong, and burns my throat going down.

And just as I suspected, I need another.

I don't think there are enough mimosas in the state of Colorado to help me out, now.

The suite is packed with people—my hairdresser, my makeup artist, a photographer, the videographer. I'm sweating like a hog. Pictures are being snapped of me in my cavewoman state and this is the furthest thing from what I expected my wedding morning would be like.

"Speed Primping! I love it!" Eva squeals with glee, her eyes gleaming with excitement.

I rip the glass away from my mouth as the photographer keeps snapping and hold up my other hand. "Ugh! No pictures! God! And turn off the fucking video!"

Everyone stops to stare at me.

"Um, please?" I add, as nicely as I can, fanning my hot face.

I'm going to pass out.

"Now, dear," my mother scolds. "We're paying them an awful lot so we might as well get our money's worth. I told them to film everything."

Right. Like I really want a memento of my nervous breakdown. "Oh. Okay. Um. Sorry. Should he come in the bathroom with me while I shower, too?"

My mother gives me a look that says she's not amused.

A bridesmaid takes the empty champagne glass, and I jump in the shower that's waiting for me.

When the shower curtain is closed and I'm truly alone, I start to bawl.

Yeah, I'm glad the photographers aren't capturing this.

I hang my head and cry so hard that I forget I need to be getting myself ready. I think of Miles. And Aaron. And how I can't stop the tears from falling on what is supposed to be the happiest day of my life.

Before I know it, I hear Eva's voice. "Lia? You okay, baby?"

I sniffle, wondering if she heard me crying. "Um, yeah."

"Well, are you clean yet? We're in a little bit of a rush, in case you didn't know!"

I look down, and I'm surprised to see that the pads of my fingers are pruning. I turn off the water and as I step out, she greets me with a towel and a fluffy white robe. "Come on, sweetie. Let's get you beautiful."

11:00 AM, DECEMBER 7

The dress is a strapless Carolina Herrera, with layers and layers of whisper-thin organza. It blows my budget and the "less is more" mantra out of the water, but like Eva said the day we bought it in downtown Denver, *when you know, you know*. There are five hundred guests waiting for me to get this show on the road. The twenty-three members of the bridal party are assembled outside the stone walkway that leads to the gazebo outside the Midnight Lodge, underneath the Rocky Mountains.

This is my fantasy.

At least, the one I'd been harboring up until today, when everything changed.

Eva smiles at me. "Ready to make your dreams come true?"

I stare at myself in the mirror. I look like Cinderella, if the wicked stepmother had just materialized at the castle on Cinderella's wedding day and gunned down Prince Charming in cold blood. I'm also about three minutes away from losing the mimosa I'd polished off earlier at breakneck speed. I go to chew on my nails but then I remember Eva painted them, and the last thing I want is for him to see the chips.

He notices things like that. He's an observer.

And I want to be perfect for him.

Him.

The wrong him.

Oh, god.

I go to chew on my lip, but I can't do that because they've been lacquered with bubble-gum pink gloss, and he'd probably notice if I got it on my teeth, too. All my normal ways of freaking out are off limits. This is the day of my dreams, and I'm not supposed to be freaking out.

But I am. Oh, lordy, am I ever.

I've been waiting my whole life for this day.

This perfect day, where the sun is shining, the snow is melting, birds are singing, and the sky is the deepest blue I've ever seen.

But there's a problem.

A problem in the form of a pretentious, bearded, six-foot-three wall of hot man flesh who stalks around hating the world and thinking he's better than everyone in it.

My fiancé's best friend. The best man, Miles Foster.

This is all his fault.

"You okay?" Eva asks.

"I am," I insist, pushing the infernal veil out of my face for the thousandth time. "This dress is itchy as hell."

I stand and pluck the dress up under my armpits, hoisting it over my boobs. I try to take a step but...too much fabric, in all directions. It's a wonder I don't drown in this sea. In this sea, or in this mess I've created for myself. I sit back down on the vanity stool and pout. "I'm stuck."

In more ways than one.

She gathers handfuls of too much organza and helps me up, depositing the pile of fabric safely in my wake. I shuffle to the full-length mirror and glance at myself. I don't look like a bride, or even a fairytale princess. I look like a prisoner who just got her death sentence.

"It's too loose," I whine. "I think I must've lost some boobage during my diet. What if the top of my dress falls down while I'm walking up the aisle?"

Eva smirks. "I'm sure Aaron'll love the show."

The thought makes the mimosa turn in my stomach. I always used to live for what Aaron thought. When I would look at something, be it a new movie coming out, or a sweater at the mall, or a new hair style, I'd think, Would Aaron like this? But I realize, as she says his name, that it doesn't matter to me in the slightest what Aaron thinks. The only opinion I care about now is that of the man who will be standing precisely two feet left of my husband-to-be.

I am such an idiot.

In less than fifteen minutes, I will be marching down the stone steps outside the Midnight Lodge to a picturesque gazebo at the foot of the hills, on the arm of my father, who has socked his entire life's savings into making this day picture perfect for his only daughter. I will take the hand of the man I've been attached at the hip to for five years, ever since I met him in a dank frat cellar when I was a wide-eyed little college freshman. I will join with this man, this man I've spent all of my adult life with, in holy matrimony, 'til death us do part.

I will become Mrs. Aaron Eberhart.

But I know I will be looking past my husband-to-be, to the man who, up until twelve hours ago, I thought I'd hated. Miles Foster.

And I will be wondering *What if...*

I wish finding a husband was as simple as finding a dress. *When you know, you know.*

I *did* know, or I thought I did. Up until twelve hours ago, I thought Aaron Eberhart was my true soul mate, the one I'd happily spend the rest of my life with. That's when things took an unexpected turn.

Right now? I don't even know my own name.

And I have a feeling I might have made a huge mistake.

"What's wrong with you?"

I peer beyond my reflection, at Eva, who's watching me suspiciously as I twist my engagement ring on my knuckle. "Um. Nothing."

"Cold feet, I suspect." Wrong. "Don't worry, once the ceremony is over, you'll feel so much better."

I will? No. Not happening.

She straightens the little tiara on my head and spreads the organza waterfall of a veil over my shoulders. "Perfect. You're a beautiful bride."

Around me, the other bridesmaids and my mother gasp in awe. The photographer snaps pictures. I try to look happy. I don't succeed.

I turn to Eva. She pats my hand but I grab it in a death grip before she can go. "I need to talk to you," I grit out under my breath. "It's important."

She can tell from the tone of my voice, I mean business. She claps her hands. "Hey, everyone. Get out. Bride needs some alone time with her maid of honor."

They all start to file out as Eva fingers my veil. She should've been in the army, with how well she can order people around. Even the photographers finally grant me some breathing room, thank goodness.

"So, what's the deal?" she asks, scrutinizing my dress to make sure there aren't any smudges on it.

"I think I'm making a mistake."

Her eyes flip up to mine. She stares at me for almost ten seconds before she laughs. "Funny."

"I'm not joking."

Her face falls. "Holy shit. You're *not* joking." She fluffs my veil on my shoulders. "But don't worry. It's not a mistake. You're fine. It's cold feet, a perfectly normal part of being a bride. You'll be—"

"I fucked Miles this morning. Is *that* normal?"

She drops my veil and nearly stumbles backwards. "You didn't."

"I did."

Her mouth takes some time to form the O it eventually settles at. I can almost see her mind cycling through potential questions.

Eventually, it lands on: "How was it?" She cringes. "No, don't answer that. I mean…how did that happen?"

I throw up my hands. "I don't know! I mean, obviously I know. We were snowbound, and at first I detested him, and then I started liking him, and then he confessed to me that he's been into me all this time. Ever since the first time we slept together. That's why he's never been with anyone else. Isn't that kind of…sweet?"

"Wait…back up." She's leaning against the vanity for support because I think I could knock her over with a feather. "The first time?"

I nod. "Yeah. Actually, it was before I met Aaron. I slept with Miles first."

Her jaw drops. "You little frat ho!" she screams.

I motion at her frantically to keep it down. My mom and all my family are right nearby.

She covers her mouth with her hands. "Whoops. And he told you he's into you? What, like, in love with you? So he's just be pining away for you for…what? Six years?"

I'm almost hyperventilating now, my heart a squished little thing in my chest. "Pretty much."

She shakes her head. "Pardon me, but does he know what a fucking asshole move that is? He couldn't have told you that six years ago? His time is up. You're marrying his best friend today!"

"I'm pretty sure Aaron's been cheating on me. All this time."

She winces. "Really?"

"Yeah. At his bachelor party. A month ago. Every time I was out of town…"

She claps both hands over her mouth again, breathing hard. "Oh, fuck."

This is the part where she'd offer me some stellar best-friend advice. I wait. And wait.

"Eva. A little advice, please?"

"Advice?" she repeats. "I can't even…holy fuck."

My shoulders slump. I know. This is awful. And the worst thing is, I did it to myself.

"All right. Here's what I think. Two wrongs don't make a right. You need to talk to Aaron and—"

"Aaron knows. He doesn't care. He wants to marry me anyway. And he promised that he'd never cheat again."

"God, Lia, are you sure? Can he really change?"

I look at her, confused.

She sighs. "You've been together five years. That has to be worth *something*. And love conquers all, right?"

I rest my head on my hands, the word *love* flashing me back to another place. Another time. Another *man*.

"But I don't know what I feel for Miles. I might...actually...not hate him as much as I thought."

"Seriously? Dahlia Marie Ripley! Have you forgotten that every time the two of you are together in the same room, you circle each other like sharks? You don't just dislike him. You abhor him! Stick with that!"

"I know, I know. I'm so fucked up."

"No. You're not. You and Miles are simply combustible. You've got a really extreme case of cold feet and freaked out in a major way. But Aaron's forgiven you. Just go and marry Aaron, Lia. That's what you've always wanted. Isn't it?"

Is it, really? Do I want the dream I've built up in my head, and am I missing out on what is truly real?

Eva tells me to go and marry Aaron. Because she doesn't *know* everything about Miles. Not the truth, the whole of it. Nor does she know Miles the way I do.

My stomach is all knotted up. "I don't know that I can do that. Miles is going to be right there beside Aaron when we're saying our vows."

She seems bewildered. "You mean that Aaron's still going to have Miles stand up for him?"

"It appears so. Bros before hos, I guess."

She laughs pitifully. "Oh, boy."

"So what do I do? I can't call the wedding off."

I look at my best friend, praying that she has some sage advice. Or a fortune ball.

Or a pair of balls I can borrow, which I will need.

Eva clucks at the mention of calling off the wedding and rubs her hands together. "No, I mean. You've been planning for years. You can't call it off, Lia." She shakes her head, scowling. "Was it really that serious with Miles?" She seems even more confused now.

I gnaw on my lip.

How can I explain everything in a minute? It would take me days to go over everything said. Every past act I misinterpreted. Every intense emotion I feel for and with Miles.

Every way Miles gets to me, not all bad, not all good, but definitely some even *better* than good.

It would take me a whole lifetime to decipher Miles. I can't even begin to explain to Eva now.

"Look, Miles really pushes your buttons, Lia. Just let that go," Eva says, clearly blaming Miles for my malady because she thinks Mr. Hot & Surly is to blame. He is: but not in the way Eva thinks. "But I think you need to talk to Miles before you walk down the aisle. Tell him that it's over, you made your decision nineteen months ago, and that you and Aaron are getting married. Tell him to leave you alone."

And then I'll give him a lap dance at the reception and shake my boobs in his face and make sure he forgets all about you," she adds, checking herself in the mirror and hoisting up her boobs so her cleavage pops out of the aqua dress.

I let out a sad laugh. "Just don't touch him."

"Oh. Of course not. Apparently only *you're* allowed to do that."

I cover my face with my hands. Flashing back to the way he let me touch him. The way we… "Oh, god." I shut my eyes, trying to shut Miles out. To get back to the present. The moment. My life back to where it was less than 24 hours ago. "You're right. I need to talk to Miles. But how? He probably hasn't even gotten off the mountain yet."

She holds up a set of car keys. They're mine.

"He's here?" I say it with so much excitement that she gives me a disappointed look.

"Yeah. Just got here about twenty minutes ago. Don't worry. I'll make it happen. I want to see you happy, Lia. This is your day! Don't let anything ruin this. Shut the fear aside and do what your heart tells you."

I sigh and hold up my hand in oath. "Promise," I say, not letting on that my heart is not happy right now and I don't know exactly why. Because my groom cheated, *again*? Or because of the best man, the man I've pined for forever and who wants me *back*?

She checks her phone. "All right. We've got to get out there before the Midnight Lodge calls this whole wedding quits on you. Ready?"

My shoulders slump. "Do I look ready?"

Because I certainly don't feel it.

She assesses me, squinting, then reaches into a box and hands me my bouquet of white gardenias. "Here. You wouldn't be a bride without it."

"Thanks," I mutter.

I've attended so many weddings where I wished I could be the bride, at the very start of a beautiful love story. And now I'd rather be anyone else.

11:16 AM, DECEMBER 7

The bridesmaids are gathered downstairs for the procession. The guests are all waiting.

There's nothing left to do but walk down the aisle.

My mother helps me with my train as I walk down the hall and to the elevator. Mimi is waiting there. "You look beautiful!" Mimi says to me as we crowd my big ol' Cinderella dress into it.

"Thank you, Mimi."

"But am I wrong, or are you not happy?"

I force a smile. "What do you mean? I'm happy. Just nervous."

"I agree." My mother gives me a sideways glance. "I know you when you're nervous. This isn't it. There's something bothering you."

Of course my mother knows. Other than Eva, my mother is my best friend. "I'm okay."

My mother scans my dress from top to bottom to make sure I'm perfect. Then she leans over and kisses my cheek. "It's never too late, you know."

"For what?"

My mother smiles. "To change your mind."

I look at both of them. They can't be serious. "Of course I wouldn't—"

"Well, your grandmother and I have been talking. And we know how some of this can seem a little like a boulder, rolling downhill. Gathering momentum until you can't do anything to stop it. But it's not."

I titter. "Oh, please. Tell that to Dad. He'd kick my ass if I backed out now."

My mother shakes her head. "He'd agree with us. The last thing he'd want is to see you unhappy. Besides, divorces are expensive, too."

Mimi nods. "And this? It's just money. It means nothing. Love? That means everything, sweetheart."

The elevator doors slide open and they're staring at me, as if expecting me to tell them something.

I wave them out the door. "Thanks for the advice. But really, the only thing I'm worried about is not tripping up the aisle. This is going to be great."

They're still eying me suspiciously, as if they don't believe me.

"Honestly! Now shoo!"

They shrug at each other. They each give me another kiss and head through the lobby, to take the arms of the ushers who are waiting to guide them to their seats. Beyond the double doors, I see rows and rows of people, dressed in their best, and the bridesmaids, all waiting for me.

This is it.

I close my eyes and suck in a breath. *You can do this. You will become Mrs. Aaron Eberhart and your dreams will come true.*

Before I can take one step, a hand clamps around my arm and draws me down a darkened corridor. I stumble over my gown and find myself in a coat closet, face-to-face with Miles Foster.

My heart starts thudding crazily in my chest.

He smells like soap and shampoo, so he must've had the time to shower. He's wearing the same gray suit I helped Aaron pick out for all of his groomsmen. I realize I've never seen him in one before. Damn him for looking so irresistibly edible.

Then I notice the angry black eye and busted lower lip. "Oh, my god. Are you—"

I try to touch him, but he flinches. "Don't. It's okay."

"No, it's—"

"It is, Lia. But don't worry. I didn't hit his face. So your pictures will be perfect."

I want to sob at how he's *always* thinking about me and what I must want. "I don't care about that!" I cry, my eyes stinging immediately.

"Look. Eva said you wanted to talk to me, and I wanted to talk to you, too. I'm sorry about everything. It was so wrong, what I did. I know that. I shouldn't have told you when and how I did. All the same, I'm not sorry I said it." He takes a breath. "I wanted you to know that after tonight, when I give the best man speech, I'm gone. I won't intrude. I'll never see you two again. All right?"

I shake my head. I know why it needs to happen, and yet every part of me is refusing. "I'll never see you again?"

"Yeah. I think I owe you two that. I've done enough damage."

I shake my head more. "No. You can't. You just can't."

He steps back and his gaze drops from my eyes, to my lips, to my dress and my veil, as if he's committing it all to memory. "God, Lia, you're the most beautiful bride I ever saw.

The most beautiful woman, period. I never stopped believing that."

More tears prick the corners of my eyes. "Miles—"

"And you *are* special. What did you say before? You needed this wedding because you had nothing else going for you?" He shakes his head. "You are everything, Lia. Sweet, kind, beautiful, smart, and a hell of a good chess player, too."

My face crumples because I'm trying not to cry. "So are you. Miles, you're—"

He hands me a handkerchief. "I'm sorry. Don't cry. I didn't mean to make you cry."

I dab at my eyes, but the waterfall is starting to flow. He's the only man who's ever had that effect on me.

I want to say a thousand things and feel like all my energy is focused on not crying right now. On not pressing into him and begging him to make everything go away.

He cups my face, then sweeps his lips over my forehead, very gently. "I wish you and Aaron every happiness," he murmurs, with such a heartbreakingly sad smile. "My two favorite people in the world."

Then he steps away from me and smooths his jacket, his tie. "I'll see you in there."

He starts to leave, his shoes sweeping on the hardwood floor, and all I can think is that I'll never see him again. He'll be walking out of my life, for good.

I can't let him go.

"Miles!" I shout, my voice hoarse. The tears are coming harder now.

He stops and turns.

"I love you," I whisper. "I love you, too."

The heartbreaking smile returns. But he doesn't say a word.

He simply turns back, opens the door, and walks away from me.

11:25 AM, DECEMBER 7

The doors open for me, and I step outside.

It's perfect weather. Mid-sixties, the sun shining high overhead. No clouds in the sky.

Eva gives me a look that silently asks, *Is all okay?* She inspects my face, grabs Miles' handkerchief from my bouquet, and starts to clean the tears from my cheeks. As soon as she does, more take their place. I can't stop.

"Shh," she says to me. "Smile. When you're walking down the aisle, just look at Aaron. Okay?"

I nod.

My father steps over to me. He looks so handsome in his suit. "I see you got a new dress for the occasion."

I laugh. My father always knew how to make me laugh, even in the darkest times.

He offers me his arm. "Ready to do this thing?"

Pachelbel's "Canon" starts to play, which is the signal for the bridesmaids to start filtering down the aisle. I peer through the curtains as each one starts to walk. There are so many guests. I never realized how many five hundred guests were. The officiant is standing in front of us, straight down the aisle. I get the briefest glimpse of my husband-to-be as the curtains part. And next to him…

Oh, god.

One by one, the foyer empties out, until Eva nudges the flower girls and ring bearer out. She gives me a thumbs-up and disappears, leaving me alone with my father.

I can't breathe.

I clutch my heart.

"Lia?" my father asks, squeezing my hand.

I draw in the air slowly and nod at him. "I'm okay. I can do this."

Pachelbel's "Canon" ends, and then the wedding march begins to play. A sound of scuffling as five hundred guests rise to their feet and turn to watch me take my last steps as Dahlia Ripley.

We part the curtains, and we begin our walk down the aisle.

It's just as I dreamed. The blue sky. The singing birds. Not a single snowflake in sight.

Yet, I almost wish there was snow.

Aaron and Miles and the rest of the groomsmen wait at the front of the gazebo. As I get closer, I can make out features on their faces. I tell myself to do as Eva said. I joke with myself that at least there are more men up there that I *haven't* fucked, than ones that I did.

I glue my eyes to Aaron's face, to Aaron's smile. I tell myself that he has truly forgotten. That we will move forward from here and build a life of mutual trust and love.

Aaron's face is red. He looks a little nervous. He pulls on his collar.

But just as Miles promised, Aaron's face is flawless.

Miles is a man of his word.

And I can't help it.

When I'm a few steps from Aaron, my eyes shift to Miles.

His gaze is on me.

And I can't seem to unstick my eyes from his.

What is wrong with me? I'm walking down the aisle, on the way to marry a man, and I just told his best friend that I'm in love with him.

I need to put the brakes on this.

This boulder, rolling downhill.

I think about what my mother said. There's always time. If I want to, I should be able to stop this.

Now.

Or, now.

My feet keep moving forward. Ankles wobbling, but moving forward, guided by my father's steady hand, as if on a track with nowhere else to go.

We reach the end of the aisle. My father steps into my line of sight to kiss my cheek.

This is the part where he'd hand me off to my husband-to-be. And he tries to.

But suddenly, I'm off the track. Pushing the boulder back with all of my might, and backing away. Shaking my head.

"I can't…" I keep whispering, mostly to myself. "I can't."

Aaron reaches for me, but I pull away. "I'm sorry. I can't do this."

In the front rows, people who've heard me start to gasp and murmur amongst themselves.

Aaron's face is tight, his lips still turned in a smile. "Lia," he murmurs. "Remember what we talked about?"

"Yeah, I do." Eva comes to my side and whispers something to me that I don't hear. I look around and see confused faces all around, and my heart begins to beat madly. My vision twists.

Everything around me is the way I envisioned, except the mountains are now closing in on me. The twittering of birds sounds like screeching. The sun is too hot.

And all of this is so wrong. Even the groom.

Especially the groom.

"Aaron," I whisper to him. "I'm so sorry. I do love you."

He pulls on the collar of his suit. "Then what's the—"

"The problem is that we're not in love!" I shout, so loudly it echoes through the mountains.

More gasps.

My eyes plead with him. "You have to know that."

He's shaking his head. "What do you mean? I thought you and I—"

"No." I look over at Mimi, in the front row, and I think of her and my grandfather, strolling down the Santa Monica pier like they were the only ones in the world. "If we loved each other, none of this would matter. But now, it's *all* that matters. And what happens after?"

He looks confused. "Well, we have our honeymoon. Hawaii."

"No. After that? This, now? It's supposed to be the easy part. I told you, Aaron, I don't know what I'm feeling. But I don't think you know, either. We got together five years ago. We were each other's first real relationship. We didn't know what we were doing.

"But now I think I understand. You know what I did was shitty and wrong, and you're willing to give me a pass, because you're a good guy. We're so used to ignoring the signals that something's wrong, because that's what we do. Maybe we need to take a step back and admit what's been screaming in our faces all this time?

"If I was in love with you, I wouldn't have needed all of this. And if you were in love with me, Aaron, you wouldn't need any last hurrah. I wouldn't be an afterthought. I wouldn't be second to your brothers or a good keg stand. I'd be at the front of your mind, all the time," I tell him. "And you're a good person. You deserve someone who comes first for you. Someone who drives you so insane with love that you can barely think. I know I'm not her."

"You *are* her. Lia—"

"No, I know I'm not. And I can't be. I don't want this."

Rage fills his eyes, and he hooks a thumb behind him. "What? Do you want *him*?"

More gasps.

I can't see Miles behind Aaron's broad shoulders, and I'm glad of that, because one look at him would probably melt me. The last thing I need is for them to throw down again in the middle of all our friends and family. "I don't know what I want! All I know is, this is a mistake."

His face is the kind of red it gets only when he's drinking. His voice is tight. "You walking out of this door is a mistake, Lia. Don't do that to me."

I shake my head, pull off the ring, and place it in his palm. "I'm sorry. Take the trip to Hawaii. You can probably bring one of your brothers."

I gather up my skirts and make a mad dash for the door.

When I get out to the front of the lodge, I'm crying so hard I can't see straight. I run straight into someone who's smoking at the entrance, and before I can move away, he grabs my hands. I look up.

"Oh! West!" I bury my face in his chest.

He tosses his cigarette on the ground and stubs it out as he wraps his arms around me. "Whoa. Dahl. What's going on? I'm not too late for the wedding, am I? I had to take a call and—"

He stops as I sob into his clean white shirt and striped tie.

"I just ran out. I can't marry him."

He smooths my hair. "Well, it's about fucking time you realized that, Peanut."

I pull away. "What?"

He smirks. "I've tried to get along with him, Dahl. But he's a fuckhead. You can do so much better."

He wipes the tears out from under my eyes as I let out a groan. "If you thought that, you could've told me sooner."

"Like you ever listen to me. Come on. Let's get you cleaned up." He wraps an arm around me and starts to walk toward the lodge, but I hold firm.

"I can't go back in there."

"Yeah? Where do you want to go?"

"Home."

"All right," he says, reaching behind me to lift my skirts. "Then let's go."

He loads me and my massive dress into his big pickup, and as I sit there in a pile of organza up to my boobs, he massages my bare shoulder. "It'll be okay, Peanut. I promise. You're a tough nut to crack."

I look over at him through a haze of tears. I feel anything but tough. I feel like I just let so many people down.

As he pulls away, I watch the Midnight Lodge fade into the distance, as well as all those fairytale wedding dreams. They don't seem to matter to me anymore.

JUNE 30TH

I step in front of the giant metal handle and take a deep breath. It's nine in the morning, my not-so-favorite time of day.

Time to open the book drop.

This branch of the Boulder Public Library, I've discovered, is a favorite among the homeless. And they're always huddling outside the front door and giving us little "gifts."

There's a reason book drop duty is reserved for the newest librarians. I can't complain, because I have a job, a real, honest-to-goodness paying job using my degree, one that I had lined up for me even before I graduated with my M.S. And I love the work, the people, the fact that I get to work with books every day, everything.

I just wish we had the budget for an intern who I could pass this particular job to.

I cringe, thinking about the human poop I received two days ago, and wondering just what wonders are in store for me today.

The door creaks as I pull it open. There, I notice books, as usual, and…great. A nondescript paper bag. Can't wait to see what's in there.

I pull it out and unravel the top, wincing, to find an empty bottle of Jack. Thank goodness it's nothing super-lethal. My friend Liz, who started working here six months before me, says that she once found a bunch of used condoms stuck to the pages of a copy of the Kama Sutra. Once she found a pile of books infested with cockroaches. And people use the drop so often as a garbage can, it's not unusual to get fast food bags and dirty diapers.

So, yeah. Proceed with caution.

"Anything good?" Liz calls over her shoulder, popping out her earbuds as she's cataloguing the new releases. She told me once she found twenty bucks that someone was using as a bookmark, so it's not all bad.

"Nothing so far."

It's been over half a year since D-Day.

I'm still single. Remarkably.

What happened after that fateful day? Well, the party went on, though without a bride and groom. My parents had sunk so much money into it that they insisted everyone have a good time. Supposedly, Aaron got shitfaced and fucked one of the waitresses behind the gazebo. Good times.

My parents didn't kill me, but they did question my sanity. As did Eva, but she eventually came around to my thinking, since she agreed Miles was irresistibly hot. So irresistible, she's fond of texting me every day to see if I've broken down and "hit that yet." Most of my friends and family were baffled. A lot of them didn't talk to me for a long time, because I'm sure they didn't know what to say. I haven't spoken to a single person in Aaron's family, either. I'm sure they all hate me.

Aaron, though?

We're still friends, weirdly enough. It helped that when he went to Hawaii with one of his frat brothers, they partied 'til they puked every night. Then, on the last day of the trip, he met this tall, gorgeous blonde named Shana who happened to be on winter break from Colorado Springs. They had a whirlwind romance, I guess, from the pictures I've seen on his Instagram. I think he's really crazy about her.

I was invited to their wedding, which was last weekend after her graduation from Colorado College, but I politely declined with regrets.

But I'm happy for him. I like to think that he's finally found *the one*.

As Miles promised, I haven't seen him since that day. I found myself staring at the Instagram photos of the wedding, not looking at Aaron and Shana, but trying to see the best man in the background. I couldn't find him. And Miles is above social media, so he might as well have disappeared off the face of the Earth.

Just like last time.

So maybe that's why I've turned down every even remotely handsome bookworm who's come into this place, asking me out.

I don't want to make the same mistake of moving on until I know that it's truly over between us.

It's been six months, though. I guess it is.

As I'm finishing up with the drop box, trying to fit the books onto the cart so I can return them to the shelves, Liz says, "Checkout."

I roll my eyes. We have self-checkout machines for this reason. "Do you need help with self-checkout?" I mumble, a little annoyed because it's so simple to operate, any idiot could do it.

"I prefer full service," a very familiar, deep voice says as I notice the title of the book he's holding. *The Alchemist.* "That's what I pay taxes for."

My eyes flash up. Way up. To him.

I gulp. "Miles! Hi!" Exhaling, I control myself, and I say, "What you pay taxes for? What are you, eighty?"

His mouth twists into a smug smile as his eyes scrape over me. "I see you're going with the full-on librarian look now, Shorty."

I look down at myself. I'm wearing a slim pencil skirt and heels, which is more dressed up than most librarians get, but it's my first month, and I'm trying to make a good impression. My hair's up in a schoolmarm bun, and I'm wearing…

Oh, god. My horn-rimmed glasses.

I start to pull them off but he says, "Don't. They look good."

I push them back up on my nose. "I thought you said I wasn't going to see you again."

He shrugs. "That was when you were marrying Aaron. I thought it was best, considering."

We stare at each other. Silent. Just looking into each other's eyes for a moment that feels like it contains everything in it.

Miles looks so good that it hurts to see him. To hear him. Smell his familiar, intoxicating scent. It's odd how my body seems to vibrate at a whole other level when he's near.

Noting he can't seem to drink me in enough too, I shake myself and I stare at the book he's holding. "This is definitely not your library. How did you know I was…"

"Aaron told me. At his wedding," he says, scratching the back of his neck. "I was his best man, remember?"

"Oh yes." I nod, my whole body singing.

"This time, though, I behaved myself with his bride." Miles winks.

He's joking, but instead of laughing, all I can do is stifle a shiver inside. Miles is so close I can... "I guess that's a good thing."

"I thought...I was hoping you'd be there."

I shake my head. "He invited me. But I thought it would be too awkward. His family pretty much hates me. How is Aaron?"

"He's good. Happy. On his honeymoon, now. And I doubt his family hates you anymore."

"Oh, well. I sent Mr. and Mrs. Eberhart an apology note, but they didn't respond. I think it's better if we all move on. Obviously Aaron has."

"Yeah. He's good."

"And we never should've been dating, much less engaged. We were pretending, because we didn't know any better."

He leans over the counter. "Do you know better now?"

I jerk my head back, meeting his gaze. "I think so." I do. Definitely. I know that no matter how much you dress it up, when it's wrong, it's wrong. I know that you can love someone without being their soul mate. And I know that no matter how odd the circumstances, when you find love, you need to hold on to it, treasure it, never let it go.

I suppose I could fill volumes with everything I've learned. But I think that maybe Miles has learned those things right alongside me, so he doesn't need the lesson. "And how are *you*?"

He shrugs and says, his voice low, "Pretty fucking miserable."

I give him a sympathetic look that tells him, I can relate. Though I've tried to pull myself together, be my own person, the miserableness of staying away from Miles while I put myself together has been acute. Compound that to the misery of thinking that I've lost him forever, that he's probably gone on with his life, after everything? And it's excruciating. But I ask, nonchalantly, "Oh. Why?"

He doesn't answer, just keeps staring at me like I already know.

My face heats. *Don't read too much into it, Lia.* I've also learned that it's important to look at things realistically rather than see them as what I think they are. So I look at the book in his hand. "That's a good book, you know. But I thought you already had it."

He studies the cover. "I do. You read it?"

I give him a sheepish look and start to gnaw on my fingernails. They're just as bad as they've ever been, and I'm sure he notices. "Um. About twelve times."

The corners of his mouth lift up in amusement. "Yeah? I've got some catching up to do, then." He peers around. "Hey. You ever get a break from this place?"

I look over my shoulder. The library isn't busy so I feel like everyone can hear us. "Um. Not until lunch."

He checks his phone. "Can I take you somewhere when you get a break? For lunch? So we can talk?"

I nod distractedly, because god, it's barely nine-thirty. I don't want to wait even a minute. "Actually, um…why don't you come with me?"

I take his book and walk past the director's office. I step out from behind the checkout desk and motion to him to follow me. When he does, I take him deep into the stacks, past rows and rows of books, to a corner of the library where we can be alone.

As we walk, he whispers, "I thought you might show up at my place. Every day. I waited for you."

My heart flip-flops. He did? I try to be casual, but I'm sure he can see my hands shaking around the book as I hold it in front of me. "I was trying to wrap my head around things. That's how I deal."

"*Ahhhh.* Sounds familiar." He smirks adorably with understanding. "Hey. And are you dating anyone?"

I smile. "I think after what I did, I'm penalized for dating anyone for the foreseeable future."

"Yeah?"

"Yeah, totally flagged. I think there should be a law about it. Girls like me should stick to the friend-zone."

I stop at the C fiction section as he leans against one of the bookshelves. "I don't think so."

"Well. I guess it wouldn't be the first time you and I disagreed." I shelve the book in the empty place he'd removed it from and narrow my eyes.

He follows my line of sight, takes the book, and turns it around so that the spine is right-side up, tsking me for the mistake. "Naughty librarian."

A shiver runs down my spine, but I try not to let it be too obvious. "Me, naughty? You're the one wasting the librarian's valuable time," I say with a hint of a wry smile. "You didn't actually come all this way for this book. Did you?"

"You caught me. I came for something else."

He's teasing me, and I'm smiling, but, all my breath leaves me as he closes the space between us, and suddenly Miles is so touchably close, that I know for sure he isn't one of the thousand dreams I've had of him since I last spoke to him. "So you're coming to return whatever it is that I left behind?"

He shakes his head, and he actually laughs. "No. I told you. I'm keeping that."

I'm frowning now. Confused.

His smile slowly starts to fade, but not from his eyes, which shine tenderly down on me. "You fucking *know,* Lia," he chides, the tone more endearing than menacing. "And if you don't know, then I may have to let you sit on it for another six months, so that you notice I've got your heart. Very, very firmly in my hands, Lia."

He waits for a moment, his gaze heated, probing, and shows me his hands. Which are big and manly and empty, but my whole chest feels full in his presence the way it hasn't in a long time, and I know that they are not empty. Not at all.

Damn him.

As always, he is right.

My voice is a breath. "And if that's true? What is it that you want from me, Mr. Foster?" I taunt breathlessly, as if my stomach isn't doing a thousand flips already.

"Why don't you take a guess?" Miles simply reaches out and tucks a strand of hair behind my ear, then places a finger under my chin and lifts my mouth to his. He kisses me, very gently, almost chastely. I taste his peppermint and feel the scratch of his beard, and I've never felt more like I was right where I belong.

This time, I don't need to guess.

When you know, you know.

3:00 PM, AUGUST 3

The dress is a *Tar-jay*, two years old, white with eyelet trim and a bit of a daring neckline, but very simple and sweet, too. I think I got it for twelve bucks on clearance, but it doesn't matter. It's his favorite. My hair is in my favorite messy bun, and my makeup is almost nil.

The locale is the musty-smelling county courthouse in downtown Boulder, right down the way from the DMV and the bail bonds office, where our officiant has just gotten done fining a guy for public drunkenness.

The details have cost us about thirty-four dollars, for the marriage license and an hour's worth of parking at the lot behind the building.

Except for the judge, we're alone.

It's my fantasy wedding come true.

Because now, everything's right.

He slips the ring on my finger, his hands trembling just as they had before, when I realized how much he loved me.

This time, I can't wait for forever. This time, there's no doubt. We will love, honor, and cherish each other, 'til death do us part.

When I'm asked if I take this man, I answer in a clear, loud voice. "I do." He says the same, his eyes never leaving mine.

And then we are pronounced man and wife.

We're fucking married!

He kisses me, and I hook my arm through his. He leads me outside, his chin up high, as proud a man as I've ever seen.

On this hot summer day, there isn't a snowflake in sight, but there *is* a cart outside, selling pretzels. He buys me one, and we sit on the steps outside the courthouse, sharing it. Of course, he lets me have the bigger piece.

"So what shall we do now, Mrs. Foster?" he asks me when I finish, and I'm licking the salt off my fingers.

We didn't make plans for a honeymoon. In fact, the plans to do this were hatched just a couple days ago. Together, we help each other embrace our spontaneous sides, and we have a lot of fun doing it. He's not that bitter old grouch who skulks around, hating everyone in the world, anymore.

I grin at him. "I like that name a lot, but that's not my real name, is it? Are you ever going to tell me who you really are, or do you prefer to remain an international man of mystery?"

"Some mystery." His eyes gleam as he leans over and whispers in my ear, "Michael Abenante."

It's a secret only he and I know. I love that he holds other people at arm's length, but lets me in, all the way. He lets me—and only me—touch him any way I please, and I think I'm going to use that to my full advantage tonight. And let him go as deep as he wants, into me.

I wrap my arms around him. "I think we should go home."

His eyes gleam with mischief. "Yeah?"

"Mmm-hmm. As good as I feel now, I think I might actually be able to beat you at chess."

"Oh, is that what's on your mind?"

"That and…other things. Maybe. If you're lucky."

"I am very, very lucky," he agrees. He pulls me close, nuzzles my neck, and whispers, "Maybe I'll let you win."

I giggle at the feeling of his breath on my ear, and people on the street smile at us, because we're laughing like school-kids and grinning from ear to ear.

Not that anything else really matters.

I love being Mrs. Foster. Dahlia Abenante. Miles' wife. Whatever I'm called, it means I'm his and he's mine. That's all there is to it. I love this man with every part of my heart, in a way that I'll probably never be able to express, in a thousand lifetimes.

And I know. I definitely just know.

DEAR READERS,

Thanks so much for reading *Best Man*. If you enjoyed it, please consider leaving a review. It helps other readers discover my stories, and spreading the love gives good karma too!

Truly hope you enjoyed Lia and Miles's complex and very human story as much as I did writing it.

XOXO,

Katy

acknowledgments

Although writing is a personal thing and sometimes quite a lonely profession, publishing is a whole other beast, and I couldn't do it without the help and support of my amazing team. I'm grateful to you all.

To my family, I love you!

Thank you Amy and everyone at Jane Rotrosen Agency!

Thank you to my editors, copy editors, proofers, and betas: Cyn, Kelli, Chanpreet, and Nina.

Thank you Nina and everyone at Social Butterfly PR.

Thank you Melissa,

Gel,

my fabulous audio publisher Simon & Schuster,

and my fabulous foreign publishers.

Special thanks to Sara at Okay Creations for the beautiful cover.

Thank you Julie for formatting,

to all of my bloggers for sharing and supporting my work—I value you more than words can say!

And readers—I'm truly blessed to have such an enthusi-astic, cool crowd of people to share my books with. Thank you for the support. xo.

Katy

about

New York Times, *USA Today*, and *Wall Street Journal*
bestselling author Katy Evans is the author of the
MANWHORE, REAL, and WHITE HOUSE series. She lives
with her husband, two kids, and their beloved dogs. To find
out more about her and her books, visit her pages.
She'd love to hear from you.

Website:
www.katyevans.net

Facebook:
https://www.facebook.com/AuthorKatyEvans

Twitter:
@authorkatyevans

Book Bub:
https://www.bookbub.com/authors/katy-evans

Sign up for Katy's newsletter:
http://www.katyevans.net/newsletter/

titles by katy evans

www.ingramcontent.com/pod-product-compliance
Lightning Source LLC
Chambersburg PA
CBHW060152180626
46813CB00007B/2710